VENGEANCE KILL

"Come on out, Raven's Egg, and we can handle this thing any way you want," said Dan Locke.

Gun smoke blossomed through the entryway as Raven's Egg, a Hudson's Bay fusee in one hand and a trade knife in the other, burst out, screaming something that resembled a cry neither human nor animal.

The shot was wide, and Locke simply stood there momentarily, aware that several Kutchins were closing in on him.

Raven's Egg rose to his full height, the single-shot fusee still smoking in his hand. He hurled the now useless weapon at his antagonist and leaped toward him.

Lucky Dan stepped to one side, pivoted, and drove his own knife through the sub-chief's heavy parka and into the flesh between his shoulder blades.

Raven's Egg dropped to his hands and knees, shuddered, and expired without a sound.

The warriors, stunned by what had happened, watched spellbound as the tall Boston, never so much as casting a backward glance, strode off toward the Hudson's Bay post.

He was whistling once again.

FIRE
IN THE
SKY

J. A. Shears

BANTAM BOOKS

TORONTO • NEW YORK • LONDON • SYDNEY • AUCKLAND

FIRE IN THE SKY

A Bantam Book / March 1988

ISBN 0-553-27071-0

Published simultaneously in the United States and Canada

Bantam Books are published by Bantam Books, a division of Bantam
Doubleday Dell Publishing Group, Inc. Its trademark, consisting of
the words "Bantam Books" and the portrayal of a rooster, is Reg-
istered in U.S. Patent and Trademark Office and in other countries,
Marca Registrada. Bantam Books, 666 Fifth Avenue, New York, New
York 10103.

PRINTED IN THE UNITED STATES OF AMERICA

KR   0 9 8 7 6 5 4 3 2 1

For Leigh and Lloye

FIRE
IN THE
SKY

... ...
... ... where I ... he will come for me. He will be

1

Red Bear's Warriors

A raven screamed.

A burst of autumn wind, cresting over the dark spruces, caused the surface of the gray-green Youcan River to rise in a series of fingerlike wavelets, and golden leaves swirled upward from clustered stands of aspen and hedges of willow. Then the air went still, and stripped leaves, suddenly lifeless, drifted onto the water's surface, coiled with the current, and slid away southward.

For the moment an uneasy sense of peace hung over the big river, and not even the omnipresent threat of Red Bear and his Koyukon warriors seemed particularly real.

Late September, the time when day and night drew equal. It had been cold that morning, with a felting of frost on everything within a quarter of a mile of the river—this matter-of-fact reminder that intense northern winter was not far off. By Christmas at Fort Youcan the sun would not rise at all, and temperatures might well be dropping to fifty below and beyond.

Lucky Dan Locke, tall, lean, and bearded, grinned as his men drove their fur-laden canoes outward from the little embarcadero at the mouth of No-Name Creek, paddles dipping smoothly into the stream. It would be a long, hard pull upriver some three hundred miles to the Hudson's Bay Company post of Fort Youcan, but the take of pelts had been good indeed. Alexander Murray, British commandant and co-director of operations, would be pleased that he'd taken the advice of a "mere Yank" and authorized this venture down the big river that flowed ultimately God-knew-where into the Russian-owned realm of Alyeska—but which in all likelihood was the very river the Russian maps dubbed the Kuikpak, flowing out of the interior and past the remote post of Nulato.

Even Fort Youcan itself, as the British were well aware, lay some significant distance into Russian-American lands, according at least to longitude and the wisdom of cartographers.

But then, of course, the Russkies had no way of knowing of this British incursion, having neither significantly explored nor even penetrated the interior of this big northern land that abutted Canadian territory.

A few more years, perhaps, and the Russians would be obliged to abandon their claims upon the North American continent—and after that, why, no doubt the Yanks and the Brits would end up settling matters between themselves.

Locke and his second in command, Hans Larsson, carried a final bale of pelts to the remaining canoe and placed it aft. Lucky Dan knelt and quickly cinched the bundled furs in place.

The raven screamed once again, and Larsson stepped out onto a big, half-submerged fir log to study the far bank of the Youcan. Possibly a couple of wolves on the prowl? Ravens always had their reasons for making a fuss.

"Ja-shu, she's good life, Daniel. Next year we got remember to bring some female-women along with us. Damn caribous, they too fast. Won' hold still. Mebbe you better steal Loon-cry away from that Raven's Egg before he whips on 'er so bad she ain' pretty no more. The lady's got eyes for ye, Dan'l, an' ye knows it's by-Gawd true. Shane, shane, a looker, Injun or not—unless 'er husband's cut up 'er face while we was. . . ."

At that moment an arrow struck Hans full in the throat, spinning him about as blood spurted from his jugular. He sprawled backward and then lay utterly still in shallow water that swirled among rounded black stones along the edge of the silt-laden Youcan.

Red Bear's men. . . .

No time to think now—no time even to worry about Hans, who had already cashed in his chips and had flat gone beaver. The danger of sudden termination was there constantly for all who ventured into the sprawling northern forests in search of furs—simply part of the bargain they all entered into.

Lucky Dan's luck was on the verge of going instantly sour—the arrow that would take him under might already have been launched, even in the instant it took to perceive some extremely narrow possible avenue of escape and launch himself down it.

He was into the canoe, driving for a swirling zone of current that might yet deliver him from quick death. At the same time he was waiting for a slim shaft of obsidian-tipped yew wood to penetrate the space between his shoulder blades, bringing with it a jolt of pain—and in that case hopefully a simple darkening of vision and then oblivion. . . . Far worse would be the option of being wounded and taken prisoner by Red Bear and his Gawddamned bloodthirsty Koyukon warriors.

Good take of prime pelts in their lands, though. . . .

The words, utterly absurd, utterly inappropriate in the present context of a man madly paddling for his life, his partner lying dead on the bank.

An arrow appeared magically a foot or so in front of where he sat straining with the paddle in his hands. The shaft scuffed against a spruce cross brace and penetrated stretched, double-layered moosehide just above the waterline—and a bit of the Youcan River began to pulse its way into the canoe.

A chorus of shouted voices behind him now—angry shouts. Then water spouted just inches from his straining right arm and was followed by the incongruously familiar dull thump of a Hudson's Bay flintlock—possibly Larsson's extra weapon, possibly . . . the Koyukons had acquired at least a few firearms from a Russian outpost off to the southwest . . . or from some other trapping brigade, whether British or Russian, who had likewise been taken by surprise.

Lucky Dan could feel the abrupt grasp of Youcan current upon his canoe. He swung the craft about, nosed downriver, and redoubled his efforts. Within moments he'd be out of range, fusees or not. . . .

He beached his canoe just up from the mouth of a large tributary creek several miles down the Youcan, stood in hip-deep water to shove the craft back under a tangle of streamside willow and huckleberry brush.

In all likelihood the Koyukons would be along directly—

as soon as one of the bastards managed to get to a canoe. No telling where they'd left their rigs—upriver probably—yes, and waited until a majority of the H.B.C. trappers were past —then the sneak attack on a single remaining canoe. Hans Larsson dead, and Dan Locke still among the living only by the grace of whatever god it was that haunted these trackless forests of spindly spruce and muskeg and mosquito-infested willow tangles.

Dan hoisted the ninety-pound pack of furs from the canoe, waded ashore, and slipped his Whitney cap-and-ball carbine through the binding straps. He checked the cylinder of his Colt Walker, thrust the gun back under his belt, hoisted the furs to his shoulders, and set off directly upslope toward a weathered formation of mudstones and aggregates that he'd investigated on a whim a couple of weeks earlier. A recessed ledge there, a recently downed cedar athwart the formation —the spot would provide excellent vantage of all that might transpire below, clear to the Youcan. Short of a massed assault by a band of twenty Indians, Lucky Dan felt confident he could hold his own as long as his ammunition held out.

As Locke scanned the forested area below him, an image of Loon-cry materialized before him and then immediately vanished. Hans had been speaking of her just before. . . .

Dan had never before been truly attracted to Indian women, though, like all men of the forest, he'd shared blankets with a few. Something about Loon-cry that was different. Fine-featured and a certain sadness about her eyes, a certain reserve and detachment—no doubt the very qualities that sometimes elicited rage and scorn in Raven's Egg, her husband. Steal her away? The wife of a powerful Kutchin sub-chieftain? Even if the woman were willing (and he had no conviction she would be), such an act could well start an Indian war—something, in fact, that Alexander Murray had made a point of mentioning to him more than once.

A hopeless love, and he knew it. An obsession, perhaps, and one that had already kept him in the Far North for a year longer than he'd even intended. He'd already saved enough money to satisfy his long-held desire to return to Missouri, to buy a little farm, to raise Hampshire pigs, to go hunting and fishing whenever he damned well felt like it. Hell, maybe even to take a wife. But then he'd seen Loon-cry—and one night he'd talked of her for hours to Hans Larsson, a night when the two of them had gotten gloriously drunk together and ended up having a shooting contest even though the both of them were so damned soused they could barely even see that big red X they'd daubed on a ragged piece of canvas to use as a target.

Hans couldn't be dead. The whole thing had to be a bastard of a bad dream.

Shit.

This venture into Koyukon lands had been deemed extremely dangerous from the beginning, and it had been nothing more than the promise of virgin trapping areas that had persuaded Alexander Murray to authorize Locke's Brigade. Contact with the Russians, of course, was to be avoided at all costs—since British presence so far westward within lands theoretically controlled by the monolithic Russian American Company might well be viewed as tantamount to an act of war. The Russian territorial governor was unlikely to make any fine distinction between the nationally owned Hudson's Bay Company and the Crown itself.

A single effective buffer between Russian fur brigades and the deep interior was the presence of unpredictable and warlike Koyukons, a people who sometimes traded with the Gossacks but who had an alarming tendency to "harvest" whatever Russians might ill-advisedly proceed inland beyond the post at Nulato on the Kuikpak River. Beyond Nulato it was open season on all men with bearded faces and white skins.

The Koyukons, Lucky Dan had argued, would provide assurance of non-contact with the Russians. Murray had nodded—yes, he remarked, but possibly the protection was every bit as hazardous as the danger.

"Rumor has it," Murray said, "that Chief Red Bear and his warriors are inordinately fond of dining on human flesh—particularly if that flesh is more or less of the European persuasion."

"Me and the boys," Locke replied, "we can handle the damned Koyukons. Just sort of nibble around the edges of their territory. Work as a group—nobody tends to his traplines alone. In any case, we'll keep a hundred miles east of the old thief's villages—work drainages where the Koyukons haven't been trapping. That only makes sense. . . ."

Indeed, all through the summer Locke's Brigade had sighted

not so much as a single Koyukon, though they had come across one recently deserted campsite. This discovery had been sufficient to cause Lucky Dan and his men to take to the river, moving operations an additional fifty miles upstream.

What was clear now: the Koyukons had themselves concluded that unauthorized strangers were at work in their lands.

Lucky Dan threw his pack of furs down and scrambled in behind, into the recessed ledge. Almost immediately he freed his carbine and settled the long barrel across the edge. He scanned the area below him, spruce and tamarack thickets extending out to the river itself. Any slight motion was suspect—any noise whatsoever, be it raven or jay or screaming eagle.

In all likelihood the Koyukons would find his hidden canoe—but what would they do after that? As skillful as he himself was at moving through the forest without leaving sign of his passing, Locke knew the Koyukons were uncannily accomplished at tracking. And when a man was running for his life, Dan reflected, he was almost certainly not as careful as he'd otherwise be.

The Indians might well assume he'd attempt to make his way to a low range of hills southward, intending to return for his canoe after the lapse of a few days—or possibly work his way back up the big river on foot.

"A decent plan, actually," Locke muttered. "But it would've meant leaving an entire pack of furs for those grinning, fish-eating bastards. . . . Bad enough that they took Hans under."

His possible survival now lay, purely and simply, in his capacity to outwit those who pursued him—for the hunter had clearly become the hunted, and safety was at least fifty miles up the Youcan, at the Kutchin village close by Tanana mouth, where his men would be waiting. If he and Hans didn't show within a day of the arrival of the others, the remainder of the brigade would move out, upstream toward the H.B.C. post. To venture back downriver would be to risk everything and would, of course, be a violation of orders he himself had issued.

The thought of just leaving Hans' body unburied was repugnant to him. If he simply outwaited the Koyukons then maybe he could return to the cove and do what was necessary.

Yes, and very likely walk directly into a trap. . . . An image came to him, that of an eagle, talons wide, striking Youcan water and rising, a writhing grayling in its grasp.

"Lucky Dan Locke," he muttered, "late of the state of Missouri, eaten by Injuns. Late. . . ."

Movement in a clearing down slope—what was it?

Half a dozen Koyukons moving along single file like so many red-legged tom turkeys on the prowl through Mississippi River glades, half a continent southward and half a lifetime past. The Indians stopped, conferred. A thick-chested fellow at the center of the group—could that be Red Bear himself?

No matter.

Cache the pack of plew right where they were and make tracks—invisible tracks, if possible.

Lucky Dan thrust the furs as far back and slipped carefully down from his temporary cover. He crouched as he moved, keeping low behind huckleberry and buckbrush thickets.

In one way or another, it was to be a footrace—his endurance versus theirs, his sense of the lay of the land against theirs.

Fifty miles to Tanana mouth. . . .

He fought to keep his mind clear as he moved—to keep his perceptions keen, his senses utterly alert. Locke breathed deeply, aware now of animal-like rhythms of his own body, his movements as he reached a faintly discernible caribou trail weaving between groves of spruce and fir and fairly well maintaining its elevation along the mountainside. The butt of his pistol pressed against his belly as he jogged easily, confident of his ability to outdistance some short-legged men who would probably not pick up his trail for another half an hour. His Whitney rifle felt good in his grasp, the faithful gun he called "Old Bull-Thrower," the very name that legendary Hugh Glass had bestowed upon his Hawken during the early days of the fur trade.

Glass, weaponless and broken-legged, chewed to hell by that grizzly sow, abandoned by his own men, had somehow made it five hundred miles down the Missouri to Fort Atkins, crawling and then limping and finally drifting on the Muddy. The saga of Hugh Glass, merely a wonderful legend until now, became far more meaningful under present circumstances. If

Old Hugh could do it, by God, and under conditions far more desperate, then Lucky Dan Locke could do it as well.

Now that he considered the matter fully, those pitiful damned Koyukons were simply no match for him. If necessary, he'd lie in wait for the bunch of them and then put them all under.

If only there were some way of doing justice to poor Larsson, some kind of half-assed burial, at least. . . .

Four days had passed by the time Lucky Dan returned to the Youcan to retrieve first his pack of furs and then his canoe. He'd angled southward away from the Koyukons and in the process had grown more and more annoyed with himself with every step he'd taken. At length he'd come to a massive landslide that had crashed to a canyon bottom a spring or two past, and there he'd found a fortresslike hollow high up amidst the rocky rubble. From such a spot, he'd concluded, he could hold off Koyukons until the cows came home.

In the meanwhile, he needed something to eat—inasmuch as his meager supply of jerked moose meat would not last long. Game was plentiful, but gunfire was out of the question. If any of Red Bear's men were within five miles or so, they'd pick up the echo. Silence, then, was of the essence. Indeed, a bow and arrow would do nicely. On the other hand, salmon were already making their way up the stream. With this purpose in mind, he wove a fish net of willow twigs laced to a forked tamarack branch, and after an hour or so became adept enough at handling the crude implement to be able to lift a pair of sockeyes from the big creek at canyon's bottom.

Fire was also out of the question, but strips of salmon flesh, half raw after an afternoon's exposure to sunlight, were sufficient to fill a man's belly.

"Hell with this," he thought, scanning the length of canyon below him. "I didn't come all the way down the Lot of Water just to turn tail. I'm going to pick up my little cache and then give Old Hans a more or less proper burying. If a man's going to go under, he might as well do it with his spurs on. No way a few pot-bellied Indians are a match for the toughest damned Yank in the North Country. Then by heaven I'll paddle to Fort Youcan and settle in for the winter. Maybe Raven's Egg will have the good grace to fall through a hole in the ice, and then Loon-cry and I. . . ."

So by early morning light on the fourth day, he came down to the Youcan, his pack of ermine, silver fox, otter, and muskrat on his shoulders. Locke cautiously approached his hidden craft. From all appearances, the Indians hadn't found it. Once satisfied his enemies were not lurking close about, Locke pulled the canoe out of its protective canopy and pushed it up onto a sandy spit. Pistol close at hand, he took time to repair the arrow hole in the canoe's prow, using rawhide lace to sew a portion of muskrat fur into place, the lacings daubed liberally inside and out with spruce sap he'd collected the previous day from a lightning-splintered tree. Only when he judged his repair job satisfactory did he load the furs aboard.

Then out onto the big river, keeping close to shore for a mile or so before tacking across gray-green water to the far bank and upstream once more.

Hans Larsson was there to greet him when he reached the cove where the H.B.C. brigade had last camped.

The body lay stretched out amid clumps of bunch grass, only a few yards from where Hans had given up the ghost and tumbled into No-name Creek's shallows. Only he didn't much look like good-natured Hans any more. Larsson's head, in fact, was no longer attached to the torso at all. It had been hacked off and was now mounted on a section of spruce branch driven into moist earth. The Hudson's Bay trapper's boots and leather breeches and jacket had been taken, and what remained was simply a headless corpse clad in red flannel underwear.

Locke resisted an impulse to vomit, steadied himself, and carried first the corpse and then its head to his canoe.

"A wonder the boys didn't roast him for dinner," Locke muttered, recalling certain unsubstantiated stories he'd been told with regard to Koyukon dietary habits. He dug the double-bladed paddle into the water and guided his craft upstream along the Youcan, keeping close to shore, Whitney carbine across his knees and at the ready.

Then he angled out toward center current, hoping to find more or less slack water to one side or the other of main current. No way of knowing where the Koyukons might be, if indeed they were within twenty miles. Their own canoes? Upstream, downstream, simply no way of knowing. In all likelihood, the Indians had tired of their search and so had headed off downriver, pleased enough to have taken the life of one Whiteman, to have acquired some clothing that wouldn't fit, a pocket watch, a compass, a pistol, a cap and ball rifle, and a few rounds of ammunition. Such tokens of victory were sufficient—so the Indians believed—and certainly preferable to a "greater" victory achieved at the cost of possible casualties. Victory, so to speak, amounted to the opportunity for exercising bragging rights. Not a matter of cowardice or anything of the sort, Locke reflected, but simply a different approach to doing business. If one dead Whiteman was sufficient to keep other Whitemen out of Koyukon lands, then one was sufficient. And if that was the case, then it was altogether possible that Red Bear and his men had actually been hoping Locke would return to bury Larsson. He, Lucky Dan, was in fact necessary to the accomplishment of Red Bear's purpose—if it was Red Bear and not simply some young bucks looking for a little excitement. Yes, the Koyukons needed him, *alive*, so that he could deliver the carefully contrived warning to Alexander Murray at the fort.

A pleasant enough thought. . . .

At this moment a pair of snow geese vaulted upward from beside a low, willow-tangled island ahead of him, their powerful wings beating through still, misty air. The birds' flight described an arc, reversing direction. Long necks thrust out, they passed back over him, startled but seemingly oblivious to his presence.

"Fly well, brothers!" Locke whispered. "This Yank'll be back in the spring—a full party with him. The Koyukons owe Lucky Dan a debt, and I'm going to collect on it. My mind's made up. . . ."

Hans Larsson's head, placed hurriedly into an empty space in the canoe's prow, had rolled over backward. A single eye was now incongruously open, and one half of the mouth was inexplicably drawn into what resembled a wry grin.

Lucky Dan Locke took a deep breath to ward off incipient nausea, flexed his fingers on the shaft of his double-bladed paddle, and dug again into muddy green water.

By noon his entire upper body was effectively numb from endlessly repetitive effort. He was already too tired even to worry about aching muscles or the blisters on the palms of his hands. No point in worrying about what couldn't be helped. Having succeeded thus far, there was little point in doing anything other than continuing to row. When necessary, pain could simply be willed away—most of it, at least.

Sundown came quickly along the river, the water's surface suddenly darkening even as the forested hills northward remained bathed in light. Then that too was gone, and gray twilight and chill air came on together, with long strands of mist rising beside willow clumps along the broad Youcan's margin.

A nearly full moon was rising eastward, almost perfectly synchronous with dying sunlight this season of the equinox. Only when the moon reached mid-heaven, Locke decided, would he cease his labors for a few hours of exhausted sleep —and preferably only if the river had the simple decency to reveal at least some small midstream island at about that time. He had no desire to find either grizzly or Koyukon grinning down at him when he woke.

Shortly before dawn Dan found a suitable island, beached his craft, and crawled back into a tangle of willow and cottonwood saplings. He slept profoundly, pistol in hand.

Morning light was gleaming from the river's surface when he came awake once more. He sat up immediately, listened intently, sniffed at the air, and rose to his feet. Then, taking time for no more than a couple of mouthfuls of badly dried fish and leatherlike jerky, he was out on the river again, now with the immediate purpose of finding a gravel bank above the Youcan—where not even heavy early summer floods would reach, a place to inter the mutilated mortal remains of Hans Larsson.

It was past midday before a site had been selected, Larsson's body and head arranged so as to appear more or less whole, and a cairn completed with a makeshift cross of rawhide-laced pieces of driftwood perched atop it. Lucky Dan stood there, beaver cap in hand, and muttered the words of the twenty-third psalm—these followed by an appeal to Raven Man, creator and death-spirit of the Far North, to see to it Hans' soul should find its way successfully across the Spirit River and into the Mystery Beyond.

Dan placed a few more stones on the heap and then lingered about uneasily for a time.

"Doesn't seem right to leave you, Hans," he said softly, "but there's no help for it. I'll stop by when I come downriver in the spring—you've got my word on it. . . ."

Locke turned and walked slowly toward the river.

"You, Boston!" a heavy voice rang out. "Hudson Bay Man!"

Lucky Dan spun, threw himself onto his chest, and leveled his pistol in the direction from whence the voice had come. A short, muscular, barrel-chested person stepped from behind a copse of twisted cedars. Elaborate headgear, salmon-skin tunic, stylized red-painted bear's head on the front—there could be no doubt as to the individual's identity.

"I am head chief of the Koyukons, Hudson Bay Man. Your people got no business down here. Stay up river with damn Kutchins, take furs there. Look. You brave man—come back and bury damned friend. My warriors all around you now—we can kill you if we want."

"They'll go home without you, friend. You're Red Bear, am I right? You even twitch, and I'll blow you to hell."

"Brave man but very stupid," the Indian replied. "Two warriors behind you right now. You be dead if I raise my hand."

"Chief, there'll be two of us dead if you do that. You the one who cut Hans' head off?"

Red Bear shrugged, grinned.

"Young men want trophy. I say, leave all of him there so you come back, find him. Do what you did."

"Damned good of you," Locke said.

"You tell them Brits—stay hell away from Koyukon land. Next time we kill damned everybody. Go home, stupid brave man. You ain't one of them. Boston Yank. But you come back, then I kill you."

With these final words, the Koyukon chief turned and walked casually back to the grove of twisted cedars, vanished from sight.

After a time Lucky Dan rose, shrugged, and strode down-slope to his canoe. Surprisingly enough, the bale of furs was still there.

Still nearly three hundred miles to Fort Youcan, and as Locke used his paddle to push out into the river, he had to fight to control his breathing.

2

Loon-cry's Husband

Dan Locke stretched his legs full-length under the rough plank table in Alexander Murray's living quarters, an area behind the high counter and in front of the warehouse of the log building which served as Fort Youcan's trading post. He leaned his back against the wall, took a long drink of thick black tea laced with H.B.C. issue brandy, and watched as the factor tallied up credit for the packs of plew Locke and his men had brought in. Across the table from him John Green Stewart leaned forward on his elbows and scowled into his own tin mug of dark brew as he spoke.

"Lucky Dan, eh?" the grim-faced Scotsman said. "That's what they call ye? Weel, laddie, I'd say ye've earned your name this trip, but I would no' push it further. I hope ye've no plan to head back down to Koyukon lands."

Locke shrugged.

"No plans at the moment beyond licking my wounds and maybe getting drunk for two or three days. Come spring, though, I figure on heading down there again. Got a debt to pay."

"Resist, Locke." Alexander Murray spoke sharply from the counter, looking up over the tops of half-lensed glasses as he wrote a final entry in the big red-bound ledger book and clapped it closed. "We've lost one good man on this venture, and that's enough. From now on you'll trap the country upriver and leave it to the natives to bring in pelts from downstream."

Locke responded in a controlled, reasoning tone.

"Koyukons mostly trade with the Russkies down at Nulato, and our friends the Kutchins are afraid to trap in Red Bear's country." Locke stopped speaking and stared into his cup for

13

several seconds, then abruptly drained it and set it on the table with a bang. "Damn it, Alexander, Hans Larsson was my friend."

"Nonetheless, I'm ordering you to leave it be. I'm sincerely sorry about Hans, Daniel, and I'm glad you escaped with your skin intact. You and your men brought in a fine take, but I was wrong to allow you to go into Koyukon lands. We don't need trouble with the hostiles now."

"Oh, hell, Red Bear's crew wouldn't stand a chance here," Locke asserted. "Half a dozen men armed with fusees could stand off the whole Koyukon nation from inside this stockade, and right now there's more than thirty of us here if you count the Kutchin trappers. Besides, I wasn't planning on bringing the bastards home with me."

The two *booshways*, as Locke and the other veteran trappers persisted in calling the company agents, glanced at one another.

"There's one thing, Danny, that ye may not be takin' into consideration," Stewart put in. "I'd admire another drop of that tea, Alexander, and a wee bit of the firewater as well. What I was saying, we can't afford to stir up a great fuss with the Indians. If the Russians catch wind of our operations here, we might be in a tight squeeze. We all know that we're not strictly in Her Majesty's domain at Fort Youcan, and the Russians wouldn't be shy about launching an attack if they find us. War with the heathen Koyukons seems likely to catch the Cossacks' attention, don't you think?"

"What I understand, the Russkies've got their hands full holding on to what they have," Lucky Dan muttered, rising to his feet. "But have it your way. It's a long time until spring, anyway. You got it all figured out how many tin mirrors and cook-pots you owe us, Alex? Guess I'll drift over to Otter Pipe's camp and visit with the old reprobate for a while. Most of my crew's there already, drinking that poison you boys cook up in the still out in the woods and losing the rest of their shares to a roll of the bones."

It wasn't late when Dan Locke stepped through the doorway of the log trading post and across to the stockade gate, but already the long Arctic twilight had settled over the outpost, a small cluster of buildings and an impressive palisade of peeled timber, the whole hunched and raw-looking against the barren low roll of brown hills and the stretch of mudflats and meandering silver ribbons of water. Furry skeins of mist hung low above the spread-out stream of the Youcan, wide and slow at this place and this time of year, the great river seeming almost halted in its flow, almost lost in the great, flat stretch of nearly featureless land.

"Flats of the Gawdamned Youcan," Dan Locke mused. "Most Godforsaken, woebegone country, surely, where human critters ever tried to live, and here's Lucky Dan. Man forgets when he's been downriver in the taiga, gets to thinking then that there's nothing in the world but trees, lodgepole and fir and no end to them ever. You forget how damned empty it can be, nothing but mudhills and swamps and little, scrubby, low-growing things that cling in the dirt. . . ."

All that, yes, but beautiful, too, a desolate, wild, uncaring beauty that can slip up on a man and catch him by the scruff of the neck and shake him, shake him until the breath goes out of his lungs and his heart swells up and seems to stop for an absolute, ringing emptiness of a moment, and he's not the same afterward. . . .

Overhead a late-traveling straggle of geese passed, their distant calls blended, almost, to a purr, the forms invisible against the dark sky, and off across the water somewhere a loon called, a drawn-out, shrieking, sobbing laugh that would surely be, Dan thought, akin to the sound with which a minor devil might greet a new arrival in hell, if such a place were more than a fairy tale. . . .

Or perhaps the cry of the newly dead, casting forth across the cold and empty earth, seeking a door back to life, lonely, lonely. . . .

"That you, old friend?" he said aloud. "I'm sorry, Hans, sorry. I know I can't make it up to you, but by God I'll do what I can."

Dan stood for a moment staring into gathering darkness, trying to catch a glimpse of the bird to convince himself that it was flesh and blood, then shrugged, turned his steps toward the cluster of hide lodges near the fort, several glowing like big lanterns from fires kindled within against rapidly encroaching darkness and chill of night; and as he drew closer, he could see as well the leaping, flickering light of a large central blaze reflected from the tops of the dwellings and could hear the singsong drone of a gambling chant, bursts of loud talk, and laughter of men at play.

"Loon-cry," he thought, hearing again the eerie yelp of the waterbird and remembering the girl with the sweet face and the strange, troubling eyes. "Hell of a name to stick on a pretty kid like that. Probably not even here anymore. . . ."

Loon-cry sat among a cluster of women who'd gathered to watch the men gambling, men squatting with intense concentration in a tight circle around a packed and smoothed area of earth and throwing bits of caribou antler marked on one side and plain on the other. Some of the women laughed and chatted among themselves, exclaiming now and again upon the cast of the bones, but Loon-cry watched in silence, hands clenched until her fingernails bit into the palms.

Raven's Egg was losing steadily and drinking the fierce trade liquor, his face gleaming with perspiration and his eyes drooping sullenly as he threw more and more of his possessions upon the pile to one side of the fire. He had long since lost the rich catch of furs—otter and marten and fox—with which he'd returned the previous day from a month-long trapping venture. Now he was wagering away their household goods. He'd already sent Loon-cry to their lodge several times to bring blankets and cast-iron pots, skinning knives, and even her prized steel needles, to throw on the growing pile.

Loon-cry watched, her face an impassive mask.

"When he has lost everything, even his traps, then he will probably wager me," she thought. "But this time I won't go. He will beat me, but that doesn't matter. He would beat me anyway, after I have been with the other man. Or perhaps I will go, and this time I won't come back, not if the other man wants me. . . ."

Things had not always been bad between them, Loon-cry recalled. When Raven's Egg had courted her, he'd been kind, an eager young man with a quick, shy smile, so much in love that he'd seemed almost afraid of her. He had married her despite his family's counsel to the contrary, for she was an orphan, her parents dead many years past of lung fever. She had nothing to bring to the union, no wealth and no family connection, for she'd been raised on the charity of various distant relatives, spending her girlhood being shuttled from one lodge to another.

His family had never been pleased with the match, particularly his father, a wily old veteran of numerous battles with the Han Indians some years earlier. The man's name was Black Claw, a cognomen received by general accord after he had single-handedly fought off a huge grizzly, losing one eye in the process and gaining an ugly scar across the left side of his face. Armed only with a knife, he'd hacked off one of the bear's toes and wore that as a badge of honor thereafter—and hence the name. Black Claw was notorious for cunning as well as for his foolhardy bravery, but everyone in the Kutchin village was aware of the bad-natured reprobate's fondness for and pride in his eldest son.

Black Claw had done his best to dissuade Raven's Egg from entering into marriage with the orphan girl, and on more than one occasion the two men nearly came to blows because of their disagreement.

At length, however, Black Claw gave in, suggesting merely that he be allowed to try out Loon-cry in bed first. When the son haughtily shook his head in denial, the scar-faced, one-eyed man merely grinned and spat upon the ground.

Yet not even Black Claw's continuing hostility had affected the couple at first. For a time they'd been happy. Raven's Egg was tender with his girl-wife, and successful as a hunter. But fortune had deserted them, and Raven's Egg had broken his leg in a fall, the injury preventing him from hunting for a full season. His relatives had given only minimal and grudging support, claiming they could afford no more, but both Raven's Egg and Loon-cry knew that the true reason for the family's miserliness was their dislike of the bride.

Raven's Egg turned bitter then, blaming Loon-cry rather than his own family for their desperate circumstances. She nursed her husband dutifully, keeping silence under his increasing vituperation and the leering rudeness of Black Claw, when that worthy occasionally paid a visit. She'd begun going to the fort the strange white men were building, washing the men's clothing and doing whatever other menial tasks they found for her to do in order to bring food and blankets and other necessary supplies to the lodge she shared with Raven's Egg.

Rather than being grateful for his wife's efforts on his behalf, however, Raven's Egg became more bitter, accusing Loon-cry of selling her body to the men at the fort. He pun-

ished her for her imagined crimes, slapping her or pulling her
hair painfully as she leaned over his sleeping pallet, once throwing
a bowlful of steaming broth at her face. But at the same time
that he abused her for her work, he insisted that she bring
him liquor with her earnings. Loon-cry endured all, telling
herself that she could not leave her husband in his helpless
state, and sure that when he was recovered he would be once
again the man she had loved and agreed to live with.

Eventually the leg healed, leaving Raven's Egg with only
a slight limp, but his spirit remained bitter. By then he'd
developed the habits of drink and of gambling, and whatever
he brought into the lodge from renewed hunting and trapping
activities went to these vices. The couple remained poor, and
Raven's Egg continued to resent and abuse his wife both men-
tally and physically—to the apparent grim delight of Black
Claw. Her life had become a nightmare; she could not leave
her husband because she had no family to return to and because
she was ashamed even to have it known that her husband
treated her badly.

Well, her shame was open now. Raven's Egg's excesses
were the subject of common gossip in the village, and although
some of the women still spoke polite greetings to her when
she saw them, she knew that when she was absent they spoke
of her either with contemptuous laughter or with pity. For her
part, she held her head higher, her spine more erect than
ever, but the wound to her pride was an ache more intolerable
to her than any black eye or bruised cheek Raven's Egg had
inflicted on her physical being.

She watched now in helpless fascination as Raven's Egg
continued his game. He won back a portion of what he had
lost, and he laughed boastfully and tossed one of his wooden
counters to Blacktail, who sat guarding a hide bucket of trade
liquor and who now passed a full dipper to Raven's Egg in
exchange for the token. Raven's Egg took two long swallows
and wiped his hand across his mouth. His unnaturally bright
gaze drifted over the noisy camp, filled now with the newly-
returned members of the Whites' trapping expedition, until
his eyes caught Loon-cry. He grinned broadly and lifted his
arm with the dipper toward her, liquor sloshing out onto the
ground.

"Loon-cry!" he shouted. "That's my woman over there,"

he explained to his gambling companions. "Fine-looking woman, isn't she? Well, I would sell her to any one of you for a pair of old moccasins. That's about what she's worth. My father told me not to take her into my lodge. She brings me nothing but bad luck. Maybe tonight you'll make it up to me, eh, Loon? In the blankets? I'll show you how I saw the bull moose do it to his cow."

He lay back laughing and Loon-cry kept her eyes fixed straight ahead, her jaw set as the heat of shame rushed into her face. She rose with straight back to return to her lodge, away from her husband and the humiliation he seemed determined to heap upon her in his drunkenness. Raven's Egg's companions pretended not to have heard anything, but as she stood up, Loon-cry caught a movement at the edge of the firelight and saw the White trapper Dan Locke take a half-step forward, fists clenched.

She had not seen him standing there with Otter Pipe before, but now their eyes met across the fire circle and held for a long moment. She'd noticed the trapper in her comings and goings at the fort, had seen that he paid attention to her in the way that men do with women. She thought him oddly handsome, with his strange, sky-colored eyes and his weatherworn face, but she hadn't thought more of him than that. Now, though, she felt as if they'd spoken many words as their eyes met across the fire, that his eyes pulled out her spirit and saw everything about her, inside and out. It suddenly seemed unbearable that Raven's Egg had shamed her in front of this man, and she dropped her gaze and turned, almost ran from the fire.

Lucky Dan's impulse had been, quite simply, to step forward and attempt to dismantle Raven's Egg when the drunken Kutchin began to humiliate his wife in front of her village. Otter Pipe, with whom he'd been talking, however, laid a hand on his shoulder to draw him back from the confrontation. But it was less the chief's gesture that had stopped him than it was the long look that passed between himself and Loon-cry. He could not say now in words what the look had communicated, but it served to freeze him in his tracks and leave him feeling short of breath.

He had little time to reflect on the matter, for Raven's

Egg rose and lurched after his woman and caught her just beyond the circle of firelight, dragging her back with one hand gripping her wrist and the other tangled in her long hair. He hesitated a moment, looking around wildly, then shoved her onto the pile of hides and trade goods that represented stakes in the game. He stood with hand raised in threat above her as he spoke.

"I have changed my mind about this woman, my friends. She is worthless to me. She is nothing but a whore. She stares and wiggles her hips at the White man and runs away from her husband. What will you wager for her, brothers? I know she isn't worth much. Elk Leggings, will you bet your lead dog for her? Your dog against my whore. That seems fair."

The man addressed shrugged uncomfortably, glanced nervously in the direction of the scar-faced Black Claw and his second son, Broken Antler.

Raven's Egg leaned over his wife in new fury, wrapped her hair around his hand and jerked her head back.

"Elk Leggings won't even risk his dog on you. Did you hear that? You bad-luck she-wolf, you whore."

Otter Pipe tightened his grip on Dan Locke's shoulder so that the White man would have to push his hand away rudely to intervene. Dan struggled to control the anger that he felt bubbling up red.

"It is not our way to come between husband and wife," Otter Pipe murmured. "Be wise, Dan Locke. There are many who hate Raven's Egg, but you are White and this is a Kutchin place. Many people believe he will come to a bad end. Let the matter take care of itself."

What happened next happened very fast, and Dan saw only a flash of fury in Loon-cry's eyes and a quick, glinting movement of her hand, and then Raven's Egg cried out and momentarily released his hold on her, clutching one wrist as blood streamed down his raised forearm.

A knife, by God she's got a knife, good for you, Loon-cry!

As Raven's Egg released his hold, the girl sprang up and tried to flee, but her husband lunged and caught her by the hair again, ignoring the wound in his arm, and pulled her to him, swung back his good arm and dealt her two hard blows to the face. Loon-cry sagged to the ground, stunned, but

Raven's Egg, still holding her by the hair, lifted his hand to strike again.

Dan Locke, unable any longer to think beyond the moment and the rage exploding inside him, shook free of Otter Pipe's restraining hand and leaped forward, catching Raven's Egg's arm before it descended. Startled, the warrior swung about to face the man who intervened. When he saw Locke, his face twisted into an ugly snarl, and his hand darted to his waist for the knife that he wore there.

Dan saw the movement, caught the arm, and with his other hand drove a heavy blow flush into his opponent's face. Raven's Egg staggered back, succeeded in drawing the knife, and lunged forward, the blade arcing upward toward Lucky Dan's face. Locke dodged the wild swipe and stepped in on the follow-through with another right, catching Raven's Egg on the jaw and jerking his head back. The Kutchin sub-chief dropped to his knees, then stumbled to his feet, but his arms didn't come up—and Dan dropped him cold with two more blows, part of his mind expecting at any moment to hear cries of fury as the entire Kutchin village erupted to the defense of its own.

You damn fool, you've done it now. This time they'll kill you sure. . . .

Instead, as Raven's Egg continued to lie sprawled on his back, unconscious but breathing heavily, the entire population of the village seemed to have been turned to stone. For a long moment there was not the slightest sound or movement. Then a collective sigh, a single breath, and a murmur as men spoke quietly to one another, some returning to neglected games, others continuing to stare at the big White.

"You had better go quickly, Dan Locke," Otter Pipe said softly, suddenly at Locke's shoulder. "Many will soon forget that they never liked Raven's Egg and will only remember that an outsider attacked one of us, a man who was disciplining his woman as is his right. One-eyed Black Claw over there, he's Raven's Egg's father—he will try to kill you one day."

Dan nodded, looked around. Loon-cry was standing, watching him also, and as if he had signaled her, she stepped forward and took his arm.

"I go with you, Boston man," she said in clear English.

* * *

"Sweet baby Jesus, Mon, what have ye let us in for now?" John Stewart asked, his face grim as he held up his whale oil lamp and stared from Lucky Dan to the pretty Kutchin girl with the vivid purple swellings on the side of her face. He wore a flannel nightshirt over red long johns, having risen from his bed to respond to Locke's insistent knocking at the trading post door. "You canno' keep the lass here. She's Raven's Egg's woman, isn't she? They do no' like us stealing their women, the Kutchins don't. They'll be attacking the fort, come morning."

"For God's sake, take her back to her husband, Locke," Alexander Murray added, leaning against the counter and yawning, "and let us get some sleep. Take him a steel axe or a Navy jacket or something by way of apology, and he probably won't even kill you."

"Can't do it, gents," Locke said. "If there's trouble, we'll clear out—head up to Selkirk or something, but she's not going back to Raven's Egg. The son of a bitch damned near beat her to death."

"Raven's Egg not my husband," Loon-cry spoke up. "I belong to Danl-ock now."

Startled, the American looked down at the girl, who had been silent since leaving the village, saw the faintest trace of a smile as she stared straight into his eyes.

"Damn it, you don't *belong* to anybody," he mumbled. "You can go wherever you want. I just don't like to see a man whipping on a woman, is all."

"Okay. I go with you."

"Stop!" Murray cried, pressing both hands to his temples. "Please. This is all very moving, chivalry in the bloody wasteland and all, but you're bringing trouble to our door. I am a damned fool to do this, but very well, Locke, keep him here. We'll probably have to kill all the natives tomorrow for it, and then we'll have no one to do our trapping, but by all means. If mighty Troy could bloody well fall for the same reason, what's our miserable little outpost to think itself above that? Madame," he added sarcastically, pulling off his nightcap and making a sweeping bow before Loon-cry, "our little Helen of the outback. . . ."

"I'm your slave forever, Al," Dan smiled.

"Of course you are. You'd best sleep back there," Murray

snapped, gesturing toward the shadowy warehouse area with its dark stacks of furs. "I don't need rioting among the men in the barracks."

It was very dark and very odorous among the bundles of fresh hides, but it was not the smell and not the faint snores drifting back from the area where Stewart and Murray slept that kept Dan awake. He pulled his blanket tighter under his chin and tried not to think about the girl wrapped in his other blanket and lying only a few inches away, a spot she'd chosen when he gestured for her to sleep where she pleased. It was difficult to ignore her, however, for she still seemed to be moving around, making soft rustling noises in the pitch blackness.

Taking her clothes off? Damn it Locke, think about something else. Like how Raven's Egg and his ugly son of a bitch of a father and all their gawddamned friends are going to sober up and come to kill you in the morning. Injuns, none of them sleep with any clothes on. Say it makes you colder. . . . Perfect little breasts, high and tipped up some, flat belly, you can tell that even with her clothes on. Acting like a fool sixteen-year-old, can't keep his mind off whatever woman happens to be closest. Only this particular female—been on my mind for a long while. . . . Now it's happened, and what in hell's this coon supposed to do? Maybe someday, but not yet. The way that son of a bitch treated her, she's not going to want to look at a man for quite a while, let alone. . . .

Dan grunted, rolled onto his side facing away from Loon-cry, closed his eyes, and felt his thoughts drift into the fuzzy incoherence that precedes sleep.

More soft sounds of movement brought him back, and the next moment Loon-cry slipped under his blanket, fitted herself against the curve of his back. Startled, he rolled over and tried to sit up.

"Loon-cry, I. . . . You don't have to. . . ."

"Lie down, Danl-ock," she whispered. "Silly White devil thing, one person, one blanket sleep here, one person, one blanket sleep there. Two people sleep together, both got two blankets. Warmer, yes? Better."

cHer fragrance was in his nostrils, her soft hair tickled his chin.

"Were you cold? Here, then, I'll. . . ."

He clumsily pulled his blanket over her, tucked it under her chin. As he did so his hand brushed across the warm softness of her breast. Naked. He pulled his hand back quickly, feeling utterly foolish and completely aroused.

"White devils sleep in clothes? You wake up cold. Here, I help you. . . ."

Dan was sure he detected a hint of teasing laughter in her voice. He lay on his back, stiff, as her hands began moving on him, seeking the fastenings on his britches.

What now, Big Man? She can't be that innocent. I feel like a damn kid, though. . . .

One hand slipped down to his belt, toyed with the buckle for a moment, then slid lower, found erect manhood, squeezed softly as she laughed under her breath.

"Good," she whispered. "I thought maybe you White devils not know what to do with woman."

And suddenly Dan Locke knew exactly what to do.

3

North Country Divorce

A month past winter solstice, and the sun had begun to inscribe the silver-white arc of its daily passage above the southern hills beyond Youcan Flats, visible now for an hour or more each cycle, with twilight extending on either side, more pronounced during those times when mists and heavy gray storm clouds were absent. But the cold was another matter, with temperatures occasionally dropping to fifty below during long nights when the aurora borealis flamed long, wavering bands of pale crimson and violet in constantly shifting patterns across the sky—so that the heavens themselves appeared to be aflame. Both Youcan River and its tributary, the Porcupine, at whose confluence the fort was situated, were solidly frozen.

Lucky Dan and half a dozen H.B.C. regulars had just returned from a day-long hunting foray. Huskies and male-mutes, now loosed from their harness, were happily gorging themselves on the fruits of their labors, and the slaughtered-out carcasses of four caribou had already been hung from a pair of overhang timbers so the meat would freeze solid during the course of the night to come. Locke's gloved hands were stiff with cold, and he was ready to rejoin Loon-cry—to take a shot of watered-down whiskey before his evening meal.

Standing at the gateway and staring back out to where the rivers joined, Lucky Dan pondered the matter of just how fish managed to survive—whether in running water beneath the ice or locked up within the ice itself.

"A hell of a trick, all right," he muttered, reaching up to free his beard of hoar frost caused by his breath. "And who'd believe damned near-hundred-degree days around here by midsummer? That's the trouble with old Raven Man—the dumb bastard lacks temperance. . . ."

Dan turned and trudged his way across packed, ice-hard snow to the fort's main building, where Alexander Murray and John Green Stewart were almost certainly to be found seated across from one another, a checkerboard between them, in front of the big fireplace—and an elk or caribou haunch dripping fat into the flames. Yes, and Loon-cry. She'd most likely be there too.

The situation with Raven's Egg had quieted to a certain extent, and the "wronged husband" appeared for a time to be adjusting to the loss of his wife despite repeated demands for revenge by the loud-mouthed Black Claw, his father—a man whose hatred for the Whites was particularly intense.

The general feeling in Otter Pipe's village, however, was one of acceptance, despite the humiliation that had been vis-ited upon Raven's Egg. Indeed, the Kutchins were quite tol-erant concerning matters of man and wife—which was to say, matters amounting to divorce. A husband was deemed to have an inherent right to beat his woman if he saw fit—so long as the woman, of her own volition, chose to remain with him. But if she put him aside, why that was a different matter—though to choose a Whiteman over a man of good family and of her own race, as Loon-cry had done, was a horse of a different color, so to speak.

But now another complication reared its head. Somehow

or another, rumor had spread to the effect that Loon-cry was pregnant. Indeed, the rumor in this case happened to be accurate. Given the absolute importance the Kutchins accorded the very idea of children, a renewal of bad feelings was bound to emerge. And that was something neither Murray nor Stewart wanted, however willing they might have been to allow their party chief to keep a squaw in his quarters.

How in hell had word gotten out?

No way of knowing that. Perhaps Loon-cry herself had allowed the information to slip during the course of some conversation or another with one of the three or four Kutchin women who had not shunned her entirely—not because she'd left Raven's Egg, but because she'd taken up with one deemed a foreigner and therefore no doubt morally inferior. At best, the Kutchins viewed H.B.C. men as a sort of necessary evil.

Touchy devils, no question about it.

Locke entered the post, savored warmth after several hours in below zero cold, and pulled off his ice-encrusted gloves. Rubbing at his mouth and beard once more, he strode toward the big fireplace where, as predicted, both Murray and Stewart were seated, just as they'd been, hardly changing posture from day to day, since perhaps the first of December.

"We got a Gawddamn world's official champion yet? And what have you worthy gents done with my woman?"

Murray and Stewart glared up at the big Yank trapper. Murray shrugged and adjusted his half-glasses.

"Bloody hell. Johnny's employing some sort of arcane Scots trickery. That or the blasted black arts. They all deal with the devil. You'll recall Macbeth, I'm sure. Either that or I can't keep my mind on the game, trying to protect a squaw-thieving American. Mr. Locke, if the Kutchins hadn't grown dependent upon company supplies to keep their operations properly afoot, we'd either be out of business or fighting the bloody savages for our very lives. How can a civilized man concentrate on checkers? As for your houseguest—what's her name? I believe she mentioned something about leaving you in favor of that good-looking Tagish brave with the broad shoulders. The one who was in to the post day before yesterday. For myself, I'd jolly well rather Bobby Campbell had never taken it into his head to colonize this patch of frozen nowhere. The man lacks judgment."

"Laddie, I'm leading Alex by twenty-two games," John Green Stewart nodded, rising, ceramic mug in hand, from the table. He strode to the big fireplace where several portions of flesh were cooking and where an oversized pot of tea hung suspended from a wrought iron hook embedded in plaster between stones. He poured, sipped at the brew, whistled softly through his teeth. "Judgin' fra' the ice on yer beetlin' brows, Daniel, I'd say ye've need of a spot o' tay. Whitemen survive in such a climate as this by virtue of monumental stupidity an' the blessing o' hot drink."

Alexander Murray stuffed a clay pipe with tobacco, lit it, puffed reflectively for a moment or two, then brought it down, glared into the bowl, stirred the mixture with a metal pick and relit it.

Locke nodded, glanced at the stuffed musk ox head mounted above the fireplace, and concluded that Johnny Stewart was no doubt more or less correct in his assessment of British presence in the far north. Brits and Yanks alike. Only it was money—furs and trade—the great and essential motivating force that drove H.B.C. operations, whatever the climate or circumstances.

"Loon-cry?" he persisted.

"In your quarters, you rock-headed Yank," Murray growled. "But I tell you, Dan, we may be having some real trouble yet. Tom Bitterman says the Kutchin braves have been talking about just who it is that *owns* the little one Loon-cry's carrying. I think it's a propitious moment for you and the lady to venture upriver to Selkirk. Then you leave her there until she's foaled."

Dan savored the odor of roasting flesh, poured himself a cup of steaming black tea, and glanced nervously toward a particular interior doorway.

Loon-cry was standing there. Yes, and he'd felt her presence even before he'd seen her.

Had she heard what Murray said?

She didn't smile, but her eyes were smiling.

"Danl-ock," she said. "I am lonely when you are gone from me. Maybe you are like the Nahoens and have taken my soul away. Come give me something else, Danl-ock."

"Shameless," Murray grumbled. "Set them up again, Johnny, you damnable Scots warlock. This time God's side takes back its own."

* * *

Loon-cry.

Who was this woman he loved? And for that matter—why was it he loved her? But it was so. He did. He had almost from the moment he'd first laid eyes on her—had, in fact, long before he himself was either able or willing to come to terms with the idea. Shortly after his initial arrival at Fort Youcan, a Yank adventurer who'd drifted north and taken employ with the British simply because the life of a trapper so thoroughly compelled his imagination that he was willing to take up company with the Brits so he could be a part of it all, yes, a part of that same mystery and freedom and drudgery and just plain excitement that had lured such legendary figures as Bridger and Beckwourth and Meek and Sublette and Carson and Smith into the wilderness twenty or so years ahead of him, the lure of the High Shining and the certain knowledge that it was possible to pit one's strength and cunning against an unforgiving wilderness and to emerge after a dozen years or so as a wealthy man. . . . But, damn it, it was a world that had somehow, for all practical purposes, vanished with the demise of the American fur trade—except in the Canadian north.

Lucky Dan Locke—"lucky" because of a hard-earned reputation for being able to take risks few others were willing to hazard and always, *always* to come up smelling like roses. But really it was that draw poker game at Fort Union, his opponent the gambler McLafferty. Damned if he hadn't drawn to a single ace and picked up three more on a final hand on which he'd ultimately bet his last blamed dollar. Mike McLafferty, convinced he was bluffing, raised him three times running and then called—the same McLafferty who'd fleeced virtually every officer and every professional card thief along the Big Muddy.

"Locke, you've got to be the luckiest bastard alive," McLafferty had said within hearing of all, and the cognomen had stuck.

Sometimes, Locke admitted, Dame Fortune momentarily glanced the other way—but somehow or another, things invariably ended up falling his way. The whole run-in with Red Bear, for instance, except for losing Hans Larsson. . . .

And Loon-cry. Even the punch that had laid Raven's Egg flat on his backside and thus enabled Dan to take Loon-cry into his quarters—the woman whose *female presence* had virtually driven him crazy was now, against all odds, his own woman—yes, and pregnant with his child.

Whatever the nature of his unwritten pact with Madame Chance was, Lucky Dan prayed she would not desert him now. Trouble was brewing, and he knew it—had known it for the past two or three weeks.

So maybe he'd been bluffing a hand again. Maybe it was time to try a new tactic before he lost the very thing, Loon-cry herself, that he desired more than anything else.

Yep, a journey to Fort Selkirk seemed to be in order. The wise man stayed the hell off slopes where avalanches were likely to occur.

It was difficult now. It was difficult, this being cut off from her own people. However brutal Raven's Egg might have been at times, at least her place within the Kutchin village had been secure, her identity and her position within a context of accepted ways of doing things and a fabric of tales and memories of the old ones and legends of beaver and porcupine and salmon and, yes, even Raven Man, that mysterious entity who acted as both protector and destroyer of her people.

This Whiteman's world that she'd entered into—a puzzling place of weapons and endless talk of trading ventures and money—there were times when Loon-cry felt she would never be able to fit in. A society of men, fierce, bearded men who seemed utterly at ease with their pistols and rifles and whatever families they belonged to away to the south at some indeterminate distance—if indeed such persons as mothers and fathers and sisters and brothers existed at all.

But Danl-ock, different from the others in a way that singled him out from them. Not a Hudson's Bay, no, a Boston—yet when she'd asked him, he told her that though Boston was a city in the country he came from, he'd never been there, that he came from a village called St. Louis that was located on a river even larger than the Lot of Water, a great river that never froze and ran through a wide flat country of grasses, a place where neither nights nor days ever grew so long as in this world where she had lived all her life and where her ancestors had lived, clear back to the time when time itself began.

The Whiteman who said he loved her and who'd risked

his life by kidnapping her away from her husband, who said
he wished to marry her and eventually to take her with him
back to that land far to the south—should she believe him?
Or would he, as her remaining women friends insisted, tire of
her and simply leave her to try to raise this child of his that
was growing within her belly? If that happened, what would
she do? More likely than not, Raven's Egg would wait his
chance and then kill her. She had no other place to go—no
parental kashim to move back into. At best, she would be
obliged to live her life as though she were some downriver
Indian within the Kutchin village. . . .

But, yes, Danl-ock was different, not like other Whitemen, and it was also true that she felt different in his presence
than she'd ever felt toward Raven's Egg or toward any of the
several Kutchin men who had at one time or another indicated
they might wish for a pretty orphan girl to share a lodge with
them. Danl-ock, something about him, his voice or those
frightening blue eyes or maybe even his smell, an odor different and strange, caused her breathing to come short and
her face to go hot so that sometimes it embarrassed her. Even
the mating act—now it was not something she did because the
man wished it but rather because she herself wished it. He
did new things to her, and even though she was fearful at
times, she wished him to do them.

Once, afterward, with Danl-ock already asleep, when she
herself was drifting away into sweet, warm darkness, she was
nearly certain she'd heard Raven Man's wings fluttering above
them, as if the dark god was motioning to her to follow him
to the entrance to that tunnel which led into the spirit world
beyond, emerging on the banks of a spirit-Lot-of-Water. She'd
gasped for breath, sat bolt upright, reached over to place her
hand on Danl-ock's bearded face, and was reassured by his
presence.

Danl-ock had strong medicine, something recognized clearly
even by Raven's Egg and the other Kutchin men in Otter Pipe's
village. For this reason no attempt had been made to steal her
back. The two White chiefs, Murray and Alexander, they knew
it too. Sometimes she listened to their talk when they were
paying no attention to her as she swept the floors or carried
in wood to the big bin close by the stone fireplace. She could
tell. They trusted Danl-ock even if they didn't always agree
with him. If there was something dangerous that needed to

be done, he was the one they asked, although he was a Boston and not a Hudson's Bay. His medicine was right there in his name. Danl-ock never said, but Loon-cry knew his totem animal had to be coyote, who was smarter than any of the other animals. Except that Danl-ock was a coyote with a brown bear's body—no, the body of a great white wolf.

She liked his body.

With the sun as high above the southern horizon as it was going to get, Loon-cry hitched a big wooden-wheeled cart to the least bad-natured of the post's mules and led the animal out through the main gate and down to the frozen Lot of Water's banks, where a great heap of split two-foot-long sections of spruce had been left by hired Kutchins who did this work in exchange for rations of dried beans or flour.

Tom Bitterman was supposed to accompany her, since Lucky Dan and three or four of the British were off on another hunting venture, but Tom was hobbling about with a case of frostbitten toes—and so she had gone alone.

When the cart was half full of wood, the mule began to puff and hiss, at the same time stamping its hooves on packed snow.

Loon-cry looked up.

Half a dozen Kutchin men were standing a few yards off, and among them were Broken Antler, Raven's Egg's younger brother, and Black Claw, the scar-faced father.

"Where your White friends, Loon-cry?" Black Claw demanded, spitting out English words with utter contempt in his voice. "They make you do their work. Maybe you better come, tend to Raven's Egg's fire. You come. Otherwise we all goin' screw you right now."

She looked immediately for some avenue of escape, but there was none. She smiled, gestured helplessly.

"Danl-ock's coming down to help me. He doesn't make me work at all. I just do things because I want to. You men throw some wood in the cart, and then I can go back to the fort."

"Whiteman's dog-woman," Broken Antler laughed. "You're not going back there. You're coming with us. Raven's Egg, maybe he's going to cut your nose off—then Danlock won't want you any more. You'll stay where you belong."

Black Claw laughed, persisted in speaking English.

"Maybe we cut nose off right now. Then nobody want you. Later we cut Danlock's little horn off, watch 'im bleed to death."

Loon-cry turned, started to run, fell. Then the Kutchin men had her. They were leading her back to their village.

Raven's Egg received his errant wife into his lodge, nodded to Broken Antler in indication of thanks, and then ordered Loon-cry to mend the sleeve of one of his fur-trimmed parkas.

Loon-cry glanced about the kashim that had once been her home. Things had clearly been rearranged. Perhaps Raven's Egg had already found some other woman—yes, that was what had happened. Who had taken her place? And where was the woman?

So now Raven's Egg thought to bring her back, degrade her as though she were some Noatagmiut slave. He would wait until after her child was born, and then he'd cast her out again, ridiculed and left to fend for herself.

Defiance in her eyes, Loon-cry backed to the opposite side of the lodge's fire pit and stared at this man who was now as a stranger to her.

"Why have you shamed me, woman?" the sub-chief demanded. "I took you as my wife, even though you were poor and no one else would have you. I have treated you no differently than other men treat their wives. I should have cut your nose off—then you wouldn't have wished to get into bed with a filthy Whiteman. Maybe I'll do that now. Are you with child, Loon-cry? That's what I have been told. You must stay here with me now, no matter what you think you wish to do. The child must have a family. It will be a Kutchin child, even though Locke is the one who sired it—or was it one of the others? How many of them have lain with you? But Whitemen cannot be trusted with children—they go away. Yes, this man will go away from you, Loon-cry. Then you'll be forced to live alone in some wretched and abandoned lodge. Who will hunt for you? Your child will starve. No, the child will belong to me. Accept your place. Obey the order I have given you."

"I have divorced you, Raven's Egg. After you beat me, I divorced you in my mind. That is a woman's right. How will you raise this child, when you lose everything you bring home playing foolish games? You paid nothing for me, and so no one

has to give anything back to you. I spit on you. When Danl-
ock finds out where I am, he will come for me. He will humiliate you once again, and my heart will be glad."

It was definitely the wrong thing to say. She knew it even
before the words had escaped her mouth—but her anger was
up, and she couldn't control it. She gauged the distance to the
lodge entryway, what her chances were of simply slipping past
Raven's Egg and fleeing from the village.

But he moved too quickly for her, a detached portion of
her mind making note that her former husband's old limp was
not in evidence at all. Within an instant he had her by the
hair and flung her to the cobbled floor of the kashim. Then,
kneeling, he grasped the front of her parka and began to back-
hand her, striking again and again.

Pain flooded through her, and consciousness began to slip
away.

Darkness and pain, but the pain was receding, was drifting
away from her.

Long twilight had faded into darkness when Tom Bitterman limped into Alexander Murray's office with word that a
band of Kutchin warriors, armed and looking for trouble, were
demanding entry to the post.

"Bloody hell," Murray said. "Is Otter Pipe with 'em? Get
the twelve-gauge off the wall and keep behind me. Thomas?
Are you deaf, man? Get a move on. Has Johnny Stewart gone
out to meet with them?"

"That he has, sir."

"And Loon-cry. Tell the woman to lock herself in her
quarters. Damn Dan Locke and his hot temper anyway. Now
the fat's in the fire, and the blasted Yank isn't even here."

"She's not in the fort, sir," Bitterman replied. "She went
for firewood, and the mule came back alone. The Kutchins
must 'ave stolen her. . . ."

Murray took off his glasses, squinted at them, and then
folded them into his pocket.

"Fine night for a bloody Indian war," he muttered.

Standoff at the gate.

Two bands of men, all of them carrying torches—and icy
mist drifting upslope from the confluence of frozen rivers. Star-

light, and wolves crying out across the nearly featureless reaches of Youcan Flats.

Murray and Stewart, backed by every H.B.C. employee on the post, made a full show of force.

"Give us Lucky Dan," Raven's Egg demanded, the smoke of his breath floating outward as he enunciated the words. "He has stolen one of our women, and now, even though she has come back, she's no good. Locke took my wife. My father and brother returned her to me, but she was no good. Now she is dead, because I have killed her. But Dan Locke is the man responsible for her death, for he's the one who defiled her. Dan Locke must pay with his life."

"Killed the lass, did ye?" John Green Stewart asked. "As I see it, chief, ye've a debt to pay Lucky Dan. What's a squaw worth these days? Best keep your friends close at hand. Here's what Alex and I can do—we'll send Locke up to Selkirk an' out o' here for aye. Then the trouble's over. Raven's Egg, perhaps ye ought best to go downriver a time—before Lucky Dan finds out what ye done and decides to ha' your hide on his wall."

"I kill this Dan Locke very soon," Black Claw snorted. "All Whitemen are cowards—hide behind their walls. Stink like shit. Locke ain't no different. . . ."

"Damned hot-tempered heathens!" Alexander Murray exploded. "Get on back to your village, now. You want to talk while the sun's still up, that'll be just fine. But you bring Otter Pipe with you—you hear me, Black Claw? Johnny and I, we'll talk with the head chief or no one. Now move on out of here, or I'll order the lads to open fire. You're good men, all of you, but no heathen devil among you shall enter the fort again until Alex and I have spoken with Otter Pipe. Be off, I say. . . ."

"Locke not here?" Raven's Egg asked. "He be standing behind you if he is here. I find him then, and after that I kill him."

"And after that, I'll hang every last rascal of you. Gentlemen, I tell you there's a nip of frost in the air. It'll be thirty below by midnight, and no time to fight a proper war. Go on back to your lodgefires now, and your fish oil and your women. Tell Otter Pipe we'll speak when the sun's up again. We'll have a spot of bloody tea and speak like civilized men. . . ."

* * *

Starlight and icy stringers of mist beside a frozen river —but it was the starlight she became aware of first. After that the mist and the river and the pain in her head. Was it possible? Had she somehow crawled through the death tunnel and not remembered it? But pain—always she'd been told the dead no longer felt pain. Was it possible, then, that she still lived?

Where was she?

She turned onto one side, flexed the fingers inside thick fur gloves but could barely discern any sensation.

Torches.

Men's voices—Kutchin voices. And Raven's Egg was among them.

So—she was alive, then. The son of a rabid wolf had carried her from his lodge and left her to the night, either supposing he'd killed her or leaving her for the cold to complete the intended murder. . . .

Loon-cry struggled to her feet, fighting back the force of inner darkness that threatened to suck her down. She stood, attempted to get her bearings.

Began to stumble forward toward the faint sensation of light emanating from behind the peeled pole stockade of Fort Youcan.

She summoned strength, then moved ahead on legs that seemed strangely detached from her.

Two days later Lucky Dan and his hunting companions returned to the fort. Tom Bitterman met him on what served as the Youcan parade grounds, and the men spoke briefly. Locke's bearded facial features went rigid.

"She's all right, though? The truth, damn it, Bitterman. Was it that son of a bitch Raven's Egg? Gawddamn it to hell. . . ."

Locke turned and strode away toward the main quarters. He entered, crossed through the big room where Murray and Stewart were once more playing checkers in front of the fireplace, nodded, mumbled a few words, and proceeded to his quarters as the two booshways rose to their feet, glanced at one another.

Then Lucky Dan and Loon-cry were in one another's arms.

An hour later the American trapper walked into Otter

Pipe's village, passing among rounded mud and hide-domed dwellings, gray smoke rising from smoke holes and dribbling away northward, blue-white and low to the ground. Those Indians who were out and about ceased whatever they were doing and, as if mesmerized, stood watching the tall man. They noted a pistol strapped to his side, and they noted that he was whistling.

Dan stopped before Raven's Egg's lodge and demanded that the occupant show his face.

"Danlock?"

"It's me, all right. Come on out, and we can handle this thing any way you want. Fists, knives, or pistols. Like I told you before, you filthy. . . ."

Gunsmoke blossomed through the entryway as Raven's Egg, a Hudson's Bay fusee in one hand and a trade knife in the other, burst out, screaming something that resembled a cry neither human nor animal, his eyes wide, his nostrils flared.

The shot was wide and Locke simply stood there momentarily, aware that several Kutchins were closing in about him.

Raven's Egg, half-crouched, now rose to his full height, the single-shot fusee still smoking in his hand. He hurled the now useless weapon at his antagonist and leaped toward him.

Lucky Dan stepped to one side, pivoted, and drove his own knife through the sub-chief's heavy parka and into the flesh between his shoulder blades.

Raven's Egg dropped to his hands and knees, shuddered, and expired without a sound.

The warriors, stunned by what had happened within the space of the preceding few seconds, moved to one side to allow Dan Locke passage between them. They watched spellbound as the tall Boston, never so much as casting a backward glance, strode off toward the Hudson's Bay post.

He was whistling once again.

Only when the Kutchin men had spoken together for several minutes was someone dispatched to inform Black Claw.

4

Down the Lot of Water

A heat wave swept over the interior during early March, and temperatures soared to a few degrees above freezing during the now rapidly lengthening days.

Meanwhile, Fort Youcan's gate was kept secured against unwanted visits by the Kutchins, and trade was held to a minimum. The situation was grave indeed, and several times Otter Pipe himself accompanied groups of men to the entryway, almost certainly at the insistence of Black Claw, to demand that Lucky Dan and Loon-cry be turned over to them. Murray and Stewart had taken the precaution of laying in all possible firewood during intervals between hostile visits, and with the firepower at the disposal of the Hudson's Bay commandants it was clear the fort was in no real danger. If anything, the Kutchins suffered most from this state of incipient conflict, since they were now deprived of some of the supplies they'd grown accustomed to. In all, the situation was serious but not desperate.

Alexander Murray and John Green Stewart continued playing checkers, having concluded that their present trouble with the Indians would pass.

In the long run, all things did. In fact, a few younger Kutchins were already bringing in furs, despite the state of undeclared war.

Locke, Bitterman, and half a dozen other veteran trappers managed to slip away from the fort unnoticed and proceeded south to make contact with outlying Han and Tanana villages with whom the H.B.C. men had not previously traded, and within two weeks Lucky Dan returned, the company dogsleds laden with respectable amounts of fur.

However, as the booshways realized, it would be ex-

tremely helpful to H.B.C. operations if they could get their
trouble-causing Yank upriver to Selkirk and keep him there
permanently. Out of sight was out of mind, and in due course
the Indians would come around. When that happened, the
reality of necessary trade would reassert itself fully.

But so long as Lucky Dan was known to be present as a
member of the stockade contingent, Black Claw and Broken
Antler were honor bound to seek revenge.

The hired trappers were uneasy—and even those who felt
kindly disposed toward Dan were talking among themselves
about the wisdom of getting their erstwhile companyero the
hell out of there.

Loon-cry had fairly well recovered from her beating and
exposure, and not even the frostbite in her left hand had proven
serious. Once she'd assured Dan she was up to the rigors of
travel, Locke himself approached Murray and Stewart and
asked permission to remove to friendlier territory.

"One thing first, however," he grinned.

"An' what might that be, laddie?" Stewart asked.

"You gents got a Bible around here? Me an' Loon-cry, we
want to get hitched proper, with the right words and all, you
understand. When we leave, we want to do it as husband and
wife."

"Ye hear this, Alex?" Stewart laughed. "It's God's own
blessin' the renegades want now."

"Bloody hell. I suppose such a thing might be arranged
at that. You Yanks actually bother to commit matrimony with
your ladies, do you?"

"Bloody yes," Lucky Dan replied.

"Is the bride willing, my young colonial friend?"

"Indeed she is."

"Aye! Dust off the bonny King James, then," Stewart
snorted.

"Bloody hell," Alexander Murray nodded.

An "official" ceremony had just been completed, and Lucky
Dan and Loon-cry were in the act of embracing one another
when the first air-shattering noise came. The trappers present
glanced toward their boss men and grinned, pounded one
another on the back.

The *Lot of Ice* was transforming itself back into the *Lot
of Water*.

Spring breakup of the Youcan ice was underway, earlier than the most ancient of the Kutchin elders could recall, but not entirely unexpected, inasmuch as large cracks had been forming for the past several days.

Now the immense power of the north country's great river exerted itself, and big plates of ice twisted up out of the water, almost as though Youcan were some immense gray-white snake in process of shedding its skin. Six-foot-thick sheets were vaulted sideways, shattering and crashing with fearful noise. Nothing less than a return to constant sub-zero temperatures could slow what was in progress.

For nearly a week the river raved and rumbled, but at the end of that time the flood, still bearing ice floes with it, was moving silently and inevitably westward, destined either for Bering Sea or Arctic Ocean, though which was as yet uncertain to the men of H.B.C., the best guess being that this was indeed the river that flowed past the Russian outposts of Nulato, Anvik, and Ikogmut—these three clearly indicated on Russian charts of Alyeska country, such as the one on the wall in John Green Stewart's office, right alongside the official British map of northern operations, the boundary line between Canada and Russian America conspicuously missing.

Travel by canoe, in any case, was once again possible.

"Danl-ock, will I like this place called Selkirk? My people have often been at war with the Tutchones and the Tagish. . . ."

Lucky Dan grinned, put his arms around his woman from behind, and squeezed her breasts.

"Right now, so to speak, they're at war with us. If we wish to have freedom to go visit the willows by the river without having a regiment along for protection, Loon Lady, then fate requires that we find friendlier neighbors. Murray says our canoe's packed and ready for us. You up for a three, four-hundred-mile frigate ride?"

Loon-cry nodded, closed her eyes, and turned her head, waiting for Dan to blow into her ear and touch her there with his tongue. She felt her pulse speed slightly with desire.

"You want me to take you into my mouth?" she whispered.

Lucky Dan laughed.

"Suppose mebbe we ought to get the rest of our gear packed first?" he asked.

Loon-cry murmured something indistinguishable in her own language, reached down to touch at the bulge she hoped she'd find beneath her man's breeches, and said, "No. . . ."

With a little time out for bad behavior, the two were nonetheless ready by late afternoon. After a supper of roast caribou haunch and baked potatoes smeared with salmon oil, Dan Locke and Loon-cry took their leave of the H.B.C. boosh-ways, Murray giving the American a highly complimentary letter to present to Robert Campbell at Fort Selkirk.

At evening twilight, then, with a full moon rimming the eastward horizon and bathing the sleeping taiga in silver, the man and woman slipped out of the fort and down to the Youcan. All was quiet, and no Kutchins were anywhere about, the last of them seemingly having retired to their village.

"Almost too easy," Tom Bitterman said, saluting clumsily as Dan and Loon-cry pushed out from the small embarcadero. "'ope your luck holds out, Yankee Dan. Say your prayers at night, an' paddle like the very devil till yer gets to the Han villages. . . ."

Lucky Dan waved and leaned into his paddle as he and Loon-cry moved out onto glittering water, on their way upriver. By morning sunlight, Dan presumed, they'd be far enough from the fort so that pursuit by the Kutchins would be fruitless.

And all went well for perhaps a mile.

Then came the blast of a fusee from out of some shadowed willow and aspen growth along the Youcan bank, no more than twenty yards distant. Simultaneously, water by the canoe's prow erupted—no, foamed up like the sudden blossoming of a pale white lily.

"Ambushed!" Dan hissed. "Turn about—turn about! The sons of bitches got wind we were leavin', lay in wait for us. . . ."

Two more shots, and then silence.

But shadowy forms were moving onto the broad river, several of them closer to shore than Locke's slim craft.

"Danl-ock! They have us cut off . . . what we goin' do? You shoot back, maybe, I'll paddle. . . ."

"And end up tipped into the drink. Damn it, damn it, I should have known. No, we've got to outrun 'em, Loon-cry. Let's turn for midcurrent, head downstream, and let the bas-tards catch us if they can."

"But we'll run past the fort, Danl-ock. What is it you want to do?"

"Downriver—downriver all the way to the ocean, if we have to. The Tanana villages or Russian posts or some Eskimo kashims, it don't make no difference. One way or the other, right now we've got to get the hell out of range. If my damned luck holds, Black Claw'll tire of the chase and go back to playing a waiting game. Because that's who it is, sure as hell. Well, the ambush tactic works both ways—if we don't catch a fusee blast or an arrow in the next few minutes. . . ."

Man and woman strained against the water, their craft knifing ahead toward where a distorted moon shimmered and retreated before them. Then they felt the full force of the Youcan's current, like God's own hands, first grasping and then realigning the canoe and speeding it down the long river.

Smoke from the big fireplace at Fort Youcan and from the Kutchin village as well lay over the water ahead of them, and then they were through it, slipping away downriver.

Emerging from mist and smoke behind were the shadows of half a dozen Kutchin canoes—but already Lucky Dan and Loon-cry had gained several hundred yards.

Somewhere ahead, Lucky Dan reflected, Hans Larsson was sleeping peacefully beside a flooding river, sheltered by a carefully placed cairn of stones—sleeping, but an un-Christly long way from his homeland. Well, perhaps that would be his fate as well, except that Black Claw wasn't likely to provide a burying. . . .

The hours drifted by interminably, darkness blending into light and then into darkness again. But by the third dawning, they were far ahead of their pursuers. Dan and Loon-cry were both on the verge of utter exhaustion. Paddling almost cease-lessly, Locke had continued down the river, past large tree-clotted islands in the broad, sometimes sluggish stream whose massive current was sometimes all but lost in its even more massive bed and the vastly greater immensity of taiga and muskeg barrens that stretched away for fifty miles in either direction. The two fugitives from Kutchin justice had stopped only for an hour's rest now and again and for the tending to natural necessity. What precious little sleep they got they took by turns, slouching forward as the westward journey continued.

The few stops were brief indeed, and then they'd push back out, always back out once again onto the river whose waters finally began to narrow, indicating that they were nearing the western extremity of Youcan Flats and so had traversed perhaps two hundred miles from the fort. Indeed, there were now low hills visible in the distance to either side of the river. Here Lot of Water was littered in places by ice ledges, tangles of downfall logs driven in against islands that formed and shifted and disappeared within the space of a few days—ice, debris, waterlogged corpses of moose and caribou, even a great brown bear quite alive and bellowing like a lost calf as it paced about on top of a log jam, for some inexplicable reason unwilling to launch itself into the heavy, silt-laden current.

Dan nudged the sleeping Loon-cry and pointed toward the stranded bear.

"A grizzly," she said. "He has no reason to be afraid of the water—why doesn't he leap in and swim to shore?"

"World's full of puzzles, Loon-love. Like for instance—how in hell'd he get stuck out there in the first place? Maybe when the ice went all at once, and he's just been hangin' on ever since."

Loon-cry sat up as they passed by the bear's log raft, waved her paddle at him.

"Great coward!" she called out. "What will happen to your woman and your little ones while you're floating down the Lot of Water?"

But the grizzly, alternating between fits of whimpering and coughing and bellowing, paid no heed to the humans who passed by in the first light of morning.

An hour or two further down, the Youcan waters grew still, overtopping the river's banks and spreading out in either direction, flooding low-lying stands of stick-spruce and spreading off to indeterminate distances over the taiga.

"Ice dam," Locke muttered. "We'll just hope to God it doesn't let go while we're paddling across it—otherwise we're in for one hell of a ride. . . ."

Loon-cry was both awake and alert now—alert with this new incipient danger. She understood well enough what would have to happen next—a portage around the jammed-up ice that blocked Lot of Water's flow and then back into the river below. And of course, should the ice dam go before they were well downstream, a crushing wall of water would come pouring with unbelievable violence behind them, and there'd be little if any chance for survival.

They heard a roaring sound ahead—the river, welling over its accumulated blockage of sheet ice, downed trees, and muddy gravels, pouring over, clouds of mist rising from beyond where the Youcan was busy gouging a new bed and at the same time eating back into the dam.

"Let's head for the south shore," Lucky Dan said. "We'll paddle in among the trees as far as we can—maybe this won't be as bad as I thought at first. Don't want you hauling things, Loon-cry, not with the little one coming. . . ."

"Kutchin women are strong," she replied. "You don't have to worry about me, Danl-ock. I carry my share. What you can do, I can do too."

Lucky Dan winked.

"Could be you're right," he said, "except in one or two matters."

She glanced back at him, her eyes strangely narrowed.

"You talk all the time—only want to keep paddling the damn canoe. Black Claw and those other men, they gave up long time ago. This way past where I ever been before. Kutchins don't come this far. They got sense—figure we're going to try to go back up river to the fort. Post a lookout along the river, maybe ten miles downstream from the village. Try to kill us then."

"Only I don't think we're ever goin' back, Loon-cry. If we do, I'll be obliged to put under half of Otter Pipe's village. . . ."

She smiled, shook her head. Danl-ock. He might even be able to do what he said. He'd killed Raven's Egg, hadn't he, and then walked right out through all the men who'd gathered around? That was what he'd told her, and he'd always spoken truth before.

The canoe slipped in through shallow water, and Dan maneuvered the craft from one open space to another under a canopy of spruce and cottonwood, avoiding rocks, snags, and submerged downfall logs. At length, however, the water was too shallow to allow passage, and Dan and Loon-cry were obliged to get out and slosh along through icy water halfway to their

knees, pulling their loaded canoe along by its tether until they'd
reached the limits of the inundated area.

Locke drew the craft up onto the still half-frozen muskeg,
unloaded, and made cache amongst a huckleberry thicket. Then
he and Loon-cry proceeded to unbind the packs containing
their belongings and to retie them into double-slinged pouches
that would fit over their shoulders. Once loaded down, the
two set off toward the Youcan ice jam, working their way to a
bluff above a sandy spit a hundred yards or so beyond the point
where the big river was safely back inside its bed.

"How long you figure that mass of ice and logs is going
to hold, Loon-cry?"

"Not long. I don't think long. Look. Big chunk over there,
it's coming loose right now. Maybe it's dangerous to go back
onto the river. I remember once when I was a girl—water got
blocked like this right where Porcupine River comes in, and
we had to move our village because the water came up there,
even right around where the fort is. Then it all goes, goes at
once, and the water went back into the river again."

Lucky Dan nodded. He too had seen ice jams break loose,
though never one the size of this.

They could leave the canoe, of course, and continue their
venture on foot—possibly even make it to safety in the Tanana
villages. Black Claw and Broken Antler, if they were still following at all, would surely not go that far. It was likely the
Kutchins had already turned back.

Another mass of ice slipped, and gouts of water roared
out. A floating log thrust through the new aperture and shot
outward, hung crazily for a moment, and then went over,
bouncing against rocks below and shattering into three seg-
ments that disappeared into boiling torrents of water and rising
mist.

"Going to be a hell of a wash if she all goes at once," Dan
said. "I'm thinking we should forget about our canoe for a spell
and wait the thing out. Take a jaunt back into the flats, maybe
even up to the first hills, see if we can take us a moose or a
caribou. Hole in someplace where we can defend ourselves
against the Kutchins, the Russians, and the H.B.C. if necessary. How say you, pretty one?"

"I say Danl-ock not much smarter than day when he was
born. Weather turn cold again, and then we freeze to death."

"Long as we're making love when it happens. . . ."

Loon-cry tried to look stern, but then she began to giggle. The tension and terrible weight of their mad flight down the river felt as though it was dropping away from her, and even their present difficult situation hardly seemed real at all. If Danl-ock wanted to take her off wandering in the taiga, why that was all right. He was strong, this one, and stupid brave. His whimsy made her feel safe once more.

"Crazy Whiteman don't know how to be serious at all. Okay. If that's the only way I can get you to . . . touch me that way again. Okay. Every day in the canoe, just running away and not stopping at all, that was no fun. We find us a big mountain maybe and climb clear to the top. First you kill my husband, and then you bring me way down here so I can freeze to death. At least Raven's Egg, he lets me freeze to death close to home."

"Didn't necessarily mean to kill him at all, for that matter. I'd have settled for cutting him up a bit—or maybe breaking a few bones."

"Still don't understand why the Kutchin men didn't cut you to pieces afterward. Strong medicine, I guess. Why don't you just *tell* the ice dam to go away? Then we can keep going wherever it is we're going. After while you get tired of paddling and then maybe. . . ."

"Thing about strong medicine, little lady, is that you've got to know how to use it. First a coon just sort of lets the ice dam know he wants it to melt out. Then he finds a nice spot back among those hills yonder, a place to build a fire where Black Claw and his henchmen can't see it. Then he gets nice and warm and drinks a bit of whiskey. And then, if he's got the right lady with him, well, he sort of gets close to her the way we've done once or twice, and then. . . ."

"What happens then?" Loon-cry asked, suddenly pressing up against him and clinging to him.

"What then? Why, I just sort of get you all excited and then turn over and go to sleep, naturally. A few days later we come back here, and sure enough, the ice dam's gone."

"No," she laughed. "I come back, you don't."

"And why would that be, pray tell?"

"Because Loon-cry cuts your throat, naturally."

"Bloodthirsty little bitch, that's what you are. Ah, God!

How simple my life was before I got hooked up with you. . . .
Well, the coyote sings when it wants to, I guess. Come along,
lass, let's head for that low ridge off to the south. Truth is, I
think Black Claw's gone home—but if we want a fire, it's safer
to get the hell back away from old Lot of Water. . . ."

"You sorry you get *hooked up* with Loon-cry?"

"Not for a minute." Lucky Dan grinned.

Loon-cry nodded, seemed satisfied.

"Okay," she said. "Maybe you tell me again about that
big river where you come from—where it don't ever freeze,
and you go to catch the fish with whiskers. You promised to
take me there some day, Danl-ock. Build a big house for me
and little ones. I'll make you keep promise—all the promises
you make me. Even ones about silk dresses and stuff. . . ."

"An' well you should. Fair enough. Right now, though,
it's best we get to movin'."

The man and the woman moved southward through the
taiga, and Locke made note that the temperature was indeed
rising, despite cloudy skies. The god of foul weather, whatever
being that was (no doubt some relative of Raven Man, the
coyote-trickster spirit of the North Country) was apparently up
to its more or less predictable tricks.

They had walked perhaps five miles from the river, and
had reached the first of a series of rises beneath a series of low
mountains at the boundary of Youcan Flats, when a fierce wind
began to blow, a warm wind that took Loon-cry's beaver cap
and sent it spinning through the air so that it lodged on a
spruce bough some thirty feet up.

"Trees like hats too," Locke muttered as he stared upward. "Just like a road sign back home—in case anyone's coming this way. Best I climb up and fetch it. . . ."

"Should have fastened the lace," Loon-cry apologized.
"This wind—storm got to be coming, a rainstorm."

Another gust blasted down from the mountains, this time
breaking limbs and snapping off the top of a tall dead snag.

Loon-cry clung to Lucky Dan, and together they struggled
away from the wind's velocity, half falling forward as they walked,
to take cover beneath a stand of young spruces.

"You not going to climb no trees, stupid Whiteman. Ain't
nobody following us—and I don't need the hat. I'll make an-

other as soon as we can camp for a day or two. Wind blows you out of the tree and kills you, and then Loon-cry and her baby all alone—nobody wants them."

Locke laughed, but the laugh was swallowed in a fury of moving air that bore with it bits of ice, particles of sand and bark, and torn vegetation.

"All right, all right!" he shouted. "Let the damned air have it then—let's take cover!"

They moved in under the protection of young spruces, and suddenly the air around them was once again relatively calm.

And it smelled different.

Rain was falling, moisture finding its way even into the darkness of the spruce thicket where they had taken shelter.

Lucky Dan hewed out a small pit in the still-frozen earth and, despite continued gustings of wind that jolted the trees about them, he was able to ignite a blaze of twigs and dry needles. After a few minutes fire was spilling over the edge of the pit and wavering along the earth like something alive, thin smoke vanishing in the drive of the wind.

Loon-cry prepared a thin soup by mixing shredded jerky into a pot of water, lodging the container into place against some stones.

"Fresh meat—that's what we need," Lucky Dan insisted. I'll be right back, most beloved of women. Maybe something's afoot out there in the downpour. Don't let the damned fire go out, now. . . ."

From under cover of the spruces, Lucky Dan strode forward into the teeth of the rain—a comparatively warm, wonderful rain that came like a cleansing, a baptism. Locke grinned, wiped moisture from his beard (realizing the futility of it) and moved toward a drainage that seemed a likely place for him to find game.

He shielded his rifle, intent upon keeping his powder dry, and then caught sight of a flash of movement a hundred or so yards ahead. He dropped to one knee in anticipation at the edge of the clearing—nodded as a pair of wolves looked up from the caribou carcass they were working on.

Locke stood up, waved his rifle, and began to run toward the wolves. The big canines gave momentary thought to defending their prey, decided instead upon the course of wisdom, and loped off toward the timber.

"You've done my hunting for me, brothers," Dan laughed.

He stooped, cut away those portions the wolves hadn't as yet gotten around to, stuffed the meat into a canvas tote bag, wiped the moisture from his face once again, and began to jog back to the thicket where Loon-cry would be waiting.

The beaver cap, he noted, had come down out of the tall tree—though he didn't see it lying about anywhere.

And that's when he sensed something was wrong. He stopped dead still, stared back the way he and Loon-cry had come in, took note as well of a muddy area downslope in the other direction, a slide mark on a low bank. It could have been a caribou that had passed through during his absence, of course, but he knew that it wasn't. The mark was human—someone had fallen.

"Those fuckin' Kutchins . . ." he whispered, pistol in hand now, backing away and at the same time attempting to recall each precise detail of the spruce copse where he'd left his woman. "I got careless—just like the day when Hans went under. . . ."

5

Black Claw's Revenge

His breath coming short, Lucky Dan scanned the ground above him. No hint of movement there, no sign of human presence at all except the skid mark in the wet earth. A swirl of wind blew the odor of smoke into his face, but in the streaming rain he could not even determine where the smoke issued from.

Damn you for the biggest fool that ever lived, Locke. Should never in the world have left her, should have known

Black Claw wasn't going to give up. How the hell could he have kept up with us? Could it be someone else, perhaps Tananas, or even Koyukons patrolling far upriver? Jesus, no. . . .

Lucky Dan felt a chill in the pit of his stomach at the new thought. Black Claw, he was sure, wouldn't hurt his errant daughter-in-law, certainly not until after the baby was born. He wanted the child. But Red Bear and the Koyukons, traditional enemies of Loon-cry's people, might do almost anything.

Locke scanned the slope again, tried to push the unwelcome thought from his mind. He moved closer to the mark on the bank, looked for footprints, but little remained to be seen, a few depressions in soft earth and even those melting in the downpour. He couldn't determine how many people had passed. The mark that he'd first noted, the heavy skid, could have been made by a person falling—that, or someone being dragged. . . .

Dan worked his way cautiously upslope, keeping to such cover as he could find, his skin twitching with the anticipation of an arrow burying itself in his hide at any instant. He forced himself to move slowly, his mind racing ahead of him as he searched for a particular stunted tree he'd noted before, one that marked the grove he and Loon-cry had taken shelter in, a spruce bent by harsh forces of nature into the form of a Z.

Bastard could have spotted me before I saw his trail, might be sitting there waiting for me, ready to jump me when I poke my nose in. Serve me right for being dumb as a post. Black Claw, it's got to be Black Claw. Even the Koyukons aren't crazy enough to go out looking for trouble in this weather.

Dan tried to convince himself of the certainty of his logic, but a terrible heaviness remained in his chest. His mind persisted in picturing Loon-cry, her beautiful face, and then transposed images of Hans, blood fountaining from his throat, and suddenly the head stuck grotesquely on a stake became that of the woman.

Locke wiped a hand across his face, swallowed, tried to clear his mind.

Loon-cry, beautiful one. We just now found each other. If anyone's hurt you, I'll. . . . Black Claw. Crazy old son of a bitch. It's got to be Black Claw. . . . Might already have taken her and gone, but I doubt it. More likely waiting to finish me. . . .

Locke scrambled up the slippery, steep ground to the edge of the spruce grove where he stood for a moment, revolver drawn. Nothing emerged, no sound but a hissing of rain, which, a detached part of his mind noted, was beginning to be mixed with slushy snow as the heavy sky darkened toward evening.

He slid into the grove silently, moved forward through wind-tossed, dripping trees, his nerves tensed for a sudden rush, a raised war-ax or knife, stunning impact and darkness if his luck didn't hold.

Nothing moved except wet branches. The odor of smoke was strong, burning his nostrils and causing his eyes to water. He blinked several times, moved in sight of the clearing.

Dan wiped his hand across his stinging eyes, at first only half believing what he saw by the light of the fire, and then he burst out laughing.

One wet-haired, blanket-wrapped figure sat holding a gun pointed at a second disconsolate and similarly attired individual, but the one holding the gun was the one with a fine-featured, delicate face.

Loon-cry turned at the sound of Dan's laughter, and she rose and smiled greetings.

"Danl-ock. I'm glad you come back. That one," she gestured with her head toward the wet, filthy, and grim-faced Black Claw, "he say I don' got to keep pointing gun, say he not goin' nowhere, but I don't trust that one."

Dan stared at her, tried to speak, found he couldn't stop laughing.

"I ain't goin' nowhere, stinking Boston. Busted arm, busted leg. Ain't goin' nowhere, hokay? No need for worthless whore daughter-in-law point gun all the damn time," Black Claw snarled.

"Still don't trust you, crazy old man," Loon-cry said.

"Rightly so, Loon-darlin'," Dan said, and then he threw his arms around her and squeezed and began chuckling again, laughter of pure relief. "You done real good. Damn, but you done good!"

In the failing twilight Locke retrieved the caribou haunch that he'd left behind when he saw the sign of Black Claw's arrival, while Loon-cry built up the fire with relatively dry wood hacked from the underside of a downed tree. With chunks of meat skewered and sizzling above the fire and a canvas groundcloth stretched into a makeshift lean-to on the down-wind side, Dan was ready to address the remarkable situation that he'd found upon his return.

"He really got a busted arm and leg?" Locke asked Loon-cry, gesturing at the sullen sub-chief.

"Don't know. Arm broke sure. Don't think leg, though. Just swole up big, all purple here," Loon-cry said, touching her ankle to demonstrate the position of the injury. "I put two sticks, what you call it? Splint. To keep arm from movin' 'round, but bones need to get put back."

"Goddamn leg busted, hokay," Black Claw muttered. "My Goddamn leg, I know if it's busted."

"Probably Loon and I ought to just waltz on out of here, leave you for the wolves," Dan remarked. "Little trade for the meat I robbed them of. But what the hell? I'm almost getting to like you, you cantankerous old son of a bitch. Let's see the damned wing first."

For a moment Black Claw looked as if he were going to refuse Locke's assistance, but when Loon-cry ordered him to allow Danl-ock to examine the injuries, he submitted, scowling fiercely into the fire.

"Broke, all right," Locke muttered, probing lightly at the swollen, discolored flesh of the arm. "Since when does Black Claw do what you tell him to?"

"I save his life, so now he's my slave," Loon-cry replied. "Has to do what I tell him."

Dan turned to stare at her in surprise.

"Saved his life?"

Loon-cry shrugged.

"Black Claw comin' up from the creek. Comin' to get me. I see him, though, I waitin' with Danl-ock's gun for him to come up. Then he slips, fall in the creek. His spirit gone away for a little while, then, he not movin', going to drown in the creek. I go down, pull him out. Now Black Claw my slave."

Dan rocked back on his heels, grinned broadly into the Kutchin sub-chief's face.

"That right, you scar-faced old bastard? She saved your

worthless hide, and now you got to do what she says? That's how it works?"

Black Claw grunted, refused to meet Dan's eyes.

Dan shrugged and turned his attention to the injured ankle, also badly swollen and empurpled. He could find no sign of a break here, however, and pronounced the problem a bad sprain. With Loon-cry assisting, Locke set the broken bone in Black Claw's arm, quite a difficult task as it turned out, requiring several minutes of wrenching and pulling. Although it was apparent that the man was in excruciating pain, Black Claw made no sound during the operation, his face set and his eyes staring straight ahead.

"By Gawd, you're a tough old bastard, ain't you?" Dan said, admiring the bad-natured Kutchin despite himself when the broken bone had at length ground and clicked into place.

Black Claw glared at him without speaking, and then, as Dan turned away for the straight branches of the splint, the old warrior's eyes rolled back up into his skull, and he fainted cold.

"Still gonna kill you, stinking White Boston devil," Black Claw growled later, revived now and chewing at a piece of partially cooked caribou meat. "Just take a little longer, that's all."

"Talk about ingratitude." Dan laughed around his own mouthful of venison. "I fixed your damned arm, didn't I? That's my meat you're eatin', too, ye old scoundrel. Don't none of it count? Besides all that, I thought ye was Loon's slave now. She don't want me killed, or is there somethin' you ain't told me, darlin'?"

Loon-cry leaned her head back against Locke's knee.

"Foolish Danl-ock. Black Claw don't kill nobody. Your life belong to me, Black Claw, and I say this."

"I kill 'im, hokay. Just take a little longer," Black Claw repeated. "Have to. My son was dishonored. I pay you back for my life somehow, worthless wife of my son, then I kill Luckydan."

"Wal, I guess I ain't that worried about it," Dan drawled, stretching out, his back against a tree. With his belly full and his clothes almost halfway dry from the warmth of the fire, he felt a glow of toleration and good will toward life in general, even toward the venomous father of the lately deceased Raven's Egg.

"How you figuring to carry out this revenge, anyhow? You ain't gonna be movin' too fast for a while, not until that ankle heals, and by then me and Loon-cry will be long gone."

"Can't leave Black Claw, Boston devil," the warrior said, a slight gleam of triumph seeming to appear in the narrow, black eyes. "Not unless you leave woman too. Now she own my life, she got to take care of it."

"That's true," Loon-cry nodded, her voice very small. "Can't leave Black Claw behind. Very serious matter to save one's life, except when shaman do it and get paid."

"Well, for . . . !"

Dan's glow evaporated. He no longer felt a particular grudge against the one-eyed old warrior, even found something perversely engaging in his single-minded avowal of revenge, threats made against all reasonable hope of carrying them through. But the notion of dragging the scoundrel with them, with his death threats and his general bad nature, was not a pleasing prospect. And by now Lucky Dan knew there was no point at all in arguing with Loon-cry on matters that touched on tradition. She would get a particular look in her eye, and logic could beat itself to death against the granite of her convictions.

Yes, the glow was definitely gone. Dan found himself, now, amongst dripping trees, sitting on sodden ground around a fire which did little to dispel the dank chill, with temperatures dropping and the prospect of a very long and uncomfortable night ahead, and not only this night but many more to be spent in the company of two rock-headed and totally unreasonable human creatures, one of whom he had the misfortune to be desperately in love with.

"You Gawd-cussed Injuns, you're all crazy as shithouse rats, you know that?" he grumbled, pulling his damp blanket around him.

Loon-cry smiled, patted at his beard.

"Is good we have wise White devil to take care of us, then?" she asked.

"Well, this particular devil says him an' Mrs. Devil are gonna make tracks out of here come morning, and if your ex-papa-in-law can't keep up, then he stays behind. We don't know but what his other kid is going to come trailing along tomorrow or the day after."

"Broken Antler turn back," Black Claw said. "Young people got no feeling for family no more. Is because of Whites, Gossacks, Bostons, Brits, make young people rotten."

"Whatever you say, Chief. Look, ye going to behave yourself tonight, or are we gonna have to sit up and watch you?"

"Don' give a damn what you do, Boston. Black Claw gonna sleep."

"What do you think, Loon-love? We could tie him up. . . ."

Loon-cry gave Black Claw a long, speculative look and then nodded.

"He be all right, Danl-ock. Is loudmouth, hothead, pretty tough, too, but not very sneaky. Not kill you in the night."

"Way I figured, too. That being the case, I guess I'll saw me some logs. I'd like to get out of here early come morning, even if it means carrying the damned canoe thirty miles around that ice jam."

The three passed a miserable night in their damp blankets and with the temperature plummeting. Even though Loon-cry and Dan slept tightly wrapped in one another's arms, the cold woke them several times—and one or another would rise to feed the fire. The afternoon's rains turned to snow in the darkness, and by morning the sleepers' blankets were coated with the white stuff while several inches covered the ground.

Outside the spruce grove, however, snow lay nearly two feet deep and still continued to fall in thick, white curtains, obscuring vision beyond a few yards in any direction. Until it let up and the soft snow either melted out or packed down, travel would be impossible.

Raven Man, it would seem, wanted him to remain in close company with the intolerable Black Claw for some time longer.

"Couldn't you of just let him drown?" he grumbled to Loon-cry, who'd stepped out of the trees behind him.

"Can't do that, Danl-ock," she said quite seriously. "Black Claw is not bad man, not really."

"Doesn't bother you that he keeps wanting to kill your husband?"

"I am not afraid," she said with a little smile. "You told me you got *strong medicine*. I believe everything you tell me."

"How we going to make love with your ex-in-law lying there scowlin' at us, tell me that, now. Of course, it don't make no difference to me. Men only do these things to please women, but they say women go crazy . . . ?"

"What things, Danl-ock?" she whispered, making her voice go husky and leaning into him. "I do not know what you speak about."

"Now cut that out, damn it," he laughed, pulling her against him. "Maybe I ought to just throw you down in the snow here. . . . "

"Maybe you should. Don' wanna go crazy."

Lucky Dan stared into her eyes, grinning, then both heard a noise behind them and turned. Black Claw stood leaning on a walking stick, glaring. He didn't speak, and after a long moment he turned and hobbled back into the shelter of the trees.

"Think he was tryin' to tell us something?" Dan laughed.

"Don't care what he think. Is very cold, Danl-ock. Let's go back to fire, put on more wood. Then we got to fix up some kind of lodge. Too damn cold here. Maybe we should go back home. . . . "

They returned to the clearing and built up the fire again. Loon-cry set a pot of melted snow-water near the flames, cut chunks of meat into it, and left it to boil while she and Dan turned their attention to the matter of housing. Both agreed that it looked to be several days before they could resume their travels, and shelter seemed a vital necessity. Locke suggested that he return to the place near the river where they'd cached their few hides as well as their canoe, for Loon-cry could easily construct a brush and hide lodge. But the trip through heavy snow would certainly take half a day, and they decided it would be wiser to make do with the material at hand—an abundance of spruce.

While Dan bent a number of springy saplings toward one another and tied their tops together, Loon-cry cut a great number of green branches. With a thick layer of these, she covered the frozen earth, and then she and Dan wove and tied a heavy thatching of green boughs to the framework of the saplings. Over one side they stretched the groundcloth, which would both serve as additional waterproofing on at least part of the structure and would cover the doorway opening.

The task took the whole of the morning, and although Black Claw kibitzed and cursed at them in the way that had by now become familiar, he seemed somewhat subdued. Loon-cry thought his injuries were perhaps giving him a good deal of pain, more than had seemed apparent the night before. Such was often the case, she knew, and she took time out from the lodge-building to slog through the snow to the stream and cut some shoots of willow, which she brewed in a tin cup by the fire into a pain-relieving tea.

Black Claw accepted the tea almost humbly when it was ready, and Loon-cry saw then that there was something else troubling the old warrior. In fact, the small gesture of kindness seemed to increase the pain in his eyes. She turned back to her work, feeling a most disturbing sense of pity for this man who had declared himself their enemy, despite his grudging obligation to her.

When the makeshift lodge was deemed complete, they gathered in a great stack of dead branches and built the fire high. The spruce thatching did a remarkably good job of sheltering them from continuing snowfall. A few flakes drifted in through the smokehole they'd left at the top of the roof and hissed to nothingness in the blaze beneath, but very little water from snow melting on the thatching seeped through. The air in the shelter became noticeably warmer, albeit rather smoky, and the springy boughs beneath made a comfortable and relatively dry bed.

Lucky Dan stretched out and sighed.

"Maybe it ain't Buckingham Palace, but I'd say it's a decided improvement, Loon-gal. What do ye say, Chief Scarface?"

Dan leaned forward as he spoke and poured a tin cup full of coffee from the pot that had been brewing, offered it to Black Claw.

"Might as well try to get along since we seem to be stuck with each other. Ye wouldn't have a pipeful of baccy, now would ye?"

Without speaking Black Claw pulled himself up and then, leaning heavily on his walking stick with his good arm, and stooping because the lodge would not permit standing, he hobbled out the entry.

Dan looked at Loon-cry, grinned.

"Now that's an improvement, too."

But when some considerable time had passed and Black Claw failed to return to the fire, the pair began to grow uneasy.

"His heart is sad, Danl-ock. Sometimes when warrior feels life no good anymore he goes, finds enemies, do crazy, brave thing so enemies kill him."

"Going to be hard put to find any enemies around here in this weather."

"Still, he might do some other foolish thing if he wishes to die. We must find him, Danl-ock."

Lucky Dan groaned, heaved himself up from his reclining position.

"Guess you're right at that. Old cuss has just gotta make things difficult. Kinda getting used to having him around, though I hate to admit it."

Black Claw was not difficult to follow, for the snowfall had eased up somewhat, and even the wiliest Kutchin would be hard-put to disguise his trail in fresh powder. Furthermore, it appeared that Black Claw was not making the slightest attempt to cover his tracks.

"Kind of looks like he wants us to catch him," Lucky Dan remarked.

"Is good sign, maybe," Loon-cry nodded. "Means he don't really want to die yet."

They followed the trail upward through the silence of a snow-laden conifer forest, the trees still carrying a heavy mantle of white. From time to time they heard the muffled roar of minor avalanches as branches shook loose their burden, but beyond that no sound, no birdsong, and very little evidence of animal activity at all beyond a few snowshoe hare tracks, one delicate trail of marten, the toes distinct. These, and the heavy, uneven track, one foot often dragging and the prints of moccasins accompanied by the hole the walking stick punched as Black Claw slogged painfully toward a ridgetop.

Once on the crest, the trail followed the ridge toward the low summit of one of the hills and from the summit back down to a rocky outcropping where wind had kept the covering of snow light. It was here that Loon-cry and Lucky Dan found Black Claw.

The old warrior lay flat on his back, his scarred, leathery

face still, one arm straight down by his side and the other in
its heavy wrappings and its red flannel sling lying across the
impressive mound of his belly.

"My God," Dan whispered, his voice instinctively hushed,
"are we too late? You can't just lie down and die like that, can
you?"

"Don't know. Black Claw have very powerful spirit, powerful will. Maybe. . . ."

"Go 'way, stinking Boston, worthless daughter-in-law. Leave
Black Claw in peace."

The Kutchin spoke without opening his eyes. The sound
of his voice made Dan suddenly feel like laughing with relief.

I'll be damned, he thought with genuine surprise. *How'd
I get to worrying so much about the surly old badger? I was
actually feeling sorry about him being dead.*

"Peace to do what?" Dan said aloud. "You just gonna stay
there until you freeze your balls off? Who the hell's gonna
avenge your kid if ye do that?"

"You must come back with us," Loon-cry added. "You're
my slave, and I order you to do this."

"Not your slave if I choose to die. I have no heart for
revenge. I am weak old man, wish to join my ancestors. Go
away now."

"Aw, come on, you scarfaced old skunk-bear. You get a
broke arm and a sore foot, and you're ready to quit. I always
figured you Kutchins wasn't very tough."

The eyes came open.

"Hokay. I get up and kill you now, Boston, if I want to,
no weapons and busted arm too. Tough enough, by Gawd. But
I don' care no more."

"Yeah? Why don't you get up and give it a try, then?"

"I know what you tryin' to do, Luckydan. But it don' work.
I don' care no more. You go way, stop bothering old man."

At a loss, Dan looked at Loon-cry. She raised her hands,
palms upward, in a gesture of bafflement.

"Look, Black Claw, why don't you just try telling us
what this is all about? If it seems like ye got a good enough
reason for doing what you're doing, then me and Loon-cry'll
leave you alone like you say you want. Otherwise we'll tie
your ass up and drag you back with us like a Gawddamned
trussed elk."

Black Claw sat up, now genuinely annoyed.

"You damn White devils can't leave nobody or nothin' alone."

"I want to know too," Loon-cry said. "All of a sudden just walk out, don' say nothing to nobody, just come away to die. Crazy."

"Yeah. I thought we was getting along pretty well—for deadly enemies, that is."

Black Claw stared at the two of them, then burst out with: "How can I live in lodge with people who kill my son, eat food with them, act like we good friends? Better die with honor."

"Hell, Black Claw," Locke countered, "I don't see anything dishonorable about it, long as you're still dead serious about meaning to kill me first chance you get."

"Got no heart for revenge no more. I tol' you that. Am weak old man and might as well die."

"What the hell do you mean you got no heart for revenge? Who's gonna hold up the family honor if you don't? I ain't likely to saunter into the village so's Broken Antler can stick a knife in me if you just up and die."

Black Claw was silent for a long moment. Then he said, "Raven's Egg was worthless son. I know that long time. Try to pretend it not so, but is true."

"Well, sure, he was worthless, all right. But that don't mean you shouldn't look out for his honor. You're his father, ain't you? What the hell kind of a father are you, anyhow?"

Black Claw considered Lucky Dan's words at length, and then, with the weary face of a man shouldering a burdensome but unavoidable duty, he pushed himself up with his stick.

"You right, stinking Boston," he said. "I come back with you, then, but remember I got to kill you sometime. I don' even want to do it no more, but is necessary."

"Sure thing," Dan nodded.

"Maybe Black Claw die of old age before he pays off debt to me," Loon-cry added, grinning at Locke.

Lucky Dan put his arm around Loon-cry's waist as they trudged downhill through the snow, Black Claw hobbling several yards behind. Suddenly Dan burst into loud laughter.

"Who'd believe that I just spent the last half-hour or so

talking like a tinhorn drummer with a monte debt, trying' to convince my sworn enemy that he ought to stay alive to kill me?"

"I believe it," Loon-cry laughed softly. "They say you Lucky, Danl-ock, not smart."

"Ah, you'll pay for that, my girl," he replied. "Just as soon as we manage to find a place for a blanket at least a couple of feet away from old Eagle Eyes. Like maybe in two, three months, you'll pay."

6

Nulato Welcome

For nearly a week snow continued to stutter down out of endlessly gray skies, and then the wind began to howl once again, the blasts at times like a great hand slapping at the spruce grove, breaking the crowns out of a few trees. When the wind left off, rain began to fall, gently at first and then gathering in intensity until it seemed as though heaven itself had burst. Moisture worked its way through the covering of their shelter, and the space inside, though kept warm by the fire, became generally humid and unpleasant.

"Damn house needs a new set of shakes," Locke muttered.

"You silly, Danl-ock. Rain not gonna keep up forever. I think storm is over by morning."

"White devils don' know how to wait," Black Claw growled. "Things never happen until Raven Man ready for them. Now you go to sleep, be quiet. Old man with broken arm needs rest. You go sit outside in rain if you wanna keep talking."

"Grouchy son of a bitch," Dan whispered to Loon-cry. "Maybe I ought to stick a knife in him—since that's what he's got planned for me in the long run."

"I like my slave," Loon-cry replied. "You leave him alone."

* * *

Warm rain now, stripping the snow from hillsides and meadows alike, and the world of Youcan River and environs seemed poised for the grand leap into springtime.

Then it sounded like thunder—intermittent, crashing and grinding, as though some sort of upheaval had begun deep underground.

"Ice dam going," Black Claw said. "Now what we do?"

"Pack our gear and watch 'er tear," Lucky Dan replied.

"Don' ask you. Talking to Loon-cry."

"Have it your own way, then. Me and the little lady, we're heading downriver to Nulato as soon as the river's safe. I suppose you're set on coming with us, ehh?"

"Whatever worthless daughter-in-law tell me. Maybe she fall overboard, an' then I save her life, an' debt all paid. . . ."

Loon-cry smiled, shrugged.

The three made their way back to the Youcan just in time to witness the entire mass of ice and logs give way—as though the river had suddenly taken it into mind to heave itself westward, overspilling its channel and ripping out entire groves of willow and spruce and poplar as it went in a massive wave of gray brown water that carried all before it.

Dan retrieved his canoe, dragging it along easily over mud-slicked earth to the river whose waters had now receded to their original limits, and within a short time he and Loon-cry had their gear lashed in place. Even with three humans aboard, Dan was pleased to note, the sturdy craft rode the water easily.

He pushed away from shore, and they were back on the stream—riding the great current of the big river of the Far North.

In no hurry now, they made camp early each afternoon, and, leaving Black Claw behind to tend to their fire, Dan and Loon-cry did what trapping they could, making a few sets and taking in the traps before leaving the following day. In the course of several hundred miles of river travel, Locke reasoned, they'd gather in enough furs at least to enable him to purchase some equipment from the post once they reached Nulato.

They stopped at the Tanana village a few miles back from that wide river's confluence with the Youcan, Chief White

Wolf's encampment, a place where he'd been received kindly the previous autumn after his confrontation with Red Bear and the damned Koyukons.

Locke strung out his traplines, enjoyed a good though brief spring hunt, and, with the days now lengthening rapidly toward summer and Black Claw's arm essentially healed and nearly as strong as ever, the three took once more to their canoe and continued their trek down the great, twisting, island-dotted river.

It was the second week in June, with darkness having dwindled to little more than an hour and gray twilight reaching out on either side, when they reached Nulato, a sizeable Yukon village complete with a small Russian stockade and a trading post.

Within minutes of drawing ashore, they found themselves confronted by three Russian soldiers carrying fusees and dressed in ragged but essentially complete uniforms.

"What the hell?" Dan muttered, but the soldiers only poked the guns at them and barked orders in Russian. When one of the trio thrust a weapon against Loon-cry's side, however, red flared inside Dan's skull, and he leapt at the man, twisting the gun from his grasp and preparing to smash his face.

Then something seemed to explode inside his head, and the world first went white, then slowly faded down to utter black.

Loon-cry watched as Vasily Deriabin, the headman of the Gossack trading post, strode back and forth in front of her, pausing now and again to cast a hard look in her direction as if to frighten some admission of guilt from her. Black Claw stood beside her in the small room in the post's main building, and the two of them were flanked by two soldiers who had escorted them into Deriabin's office and had prodded the Kutchin war chief's ribs with a gun barrel when he began shouting at the agent, demanding to know what they had done with "that Goddamn Luckydan." Now Black Claw kept silence, but he returned Deriabin's looks with a fiercely belligerent glare. Loon-cry tried to stand tall, to adopt the wooden, masklike expression she'd learned to employ when she was Raven's Egg's wife, but she couldn't seem to stop her knees from trembling.

Where is Danl-ock? she wanted to scream. *What have you done with him? If he is dead, then I no longer wish to live.*

Nothing had seemed real since the moment when they'd stepped ashore and the Gossack soldiers had pointed guns at them and then struck Danl-ock. She'd watched, utterly helpless, as two of the soldiers dragged his inert form away and the other, waving his weapon, had forced her and Black Claw to march ahead of him into this place, which she recognized as being similar in many respects to the Hudson's Bay trading post at Fort Youcan. Thus, she reasoned, the man who'd been sitting behind the desk moving papers around when they came in, the same man who now strode back and forth before them, must fulfill a similar function to Alexander Murray's. But Murray had always been kind to her, when he noticed her at all. This man, however, was angry, and she did not even know why.

Deriabin listened to the soldiers' report in silence, staring at the two before him, and then he dispatched one of them, the two speaking the Gossack language. Loon-cry recognized a few words from the trading patois, used by all the tribes and made up of words from many tongues, but not enough to understand anything that was said. Deriabin continued his silent pacing.

In a few minutes the soldier returned with a man in an ornate blue coat, somewhat stained and rumpled, but still splendid with gold braid and brass buttons, and if Loon-cry judged his expression correctly, he looked more worried than angry, his face perhaps even kind.

"What's this about, Deriabin?" the newcomer asked in English—English that to Loon-cry sounded similar to the kind that Alexander Murray spoke rather than the kind Danl-ock used. "Your man tried to explain it to me, but he has very little English, and I'm afraid I have even less Russian. Something about an H.B.C. trapper coming here, if I heard correctly?"

"Is correct, Lieutenant Bernard. They came down in canoe from somewhere upriver on the Kuikpak. Speaks English, has many British trade goods, Hudson's Bay blankets, British fusee, an American pistol and rifle. Also has two packs of furs. *Nyee kahrahsho*, Lieutenant. I think these are furs stolen from Russian lands. You know something about this, perhaps?"

"Not a blessed notion. If such a man came down the river, then very likely the Kuikpak arises in the territory of Canada, just as you've surmised. I have nothing to do with the H.B.C., as you know. My mission here is simply . . ."

"*Nyee zah shto*, I know what you said your mission is. Now I wonder. I wonder if British are moving into Russian lands. You know about such a thing, Lieutenant?"

"Now see here, *Mister* Deriabin . . ." the British officer began, and then visibly checked his anger and started over again. "I assure you my mission is as I said. I'm simply trying to discover what happened to my countryman Franklin and his men after their ship went down, and I'm most grateful for your cooperation, both personally and in behalf of Her Majesty's Navy. It would seem more to the point to question the trapper, don't you think? You have him in custody somewhere, I presume? And who are these two natives? They have something to do with the matter?"

"*Da, da.* The *angleeski* trapper is in safekeeping. These two were with him in the boat. I will talk to the trapper in good time. For now, we let him rest a bit, think about things while I find out what these two know."

"Deriabin, I should warn you that detaining a British subject anywhere on earth is a serious matter. . . ."

"Luckydan ain't no Goddam Brit," Black Claw snorted.

Both the Russian factor and the English naval officer turned to stare at the Kutchin as if the doorpost had interrupted their disagreement. One of the soldiers prodded halfheartedly at Black Claw's ribs with his weapon, but Deriabin raised his hand in sign for the man to desist.

"I forget you speak *angleeski*," Deriabin said. "What do you mean this Luckydan is no *Brit*? What tribe are you from, anyway, and who is this woman? You dress differently than the people we trade with."

"I am Black Claw, war chief of Kutchins," the scar-faced one said, drawing himself up proudly. "I say Luckydan no Hudson Bay, no Goddam Brit. Is stinking Boston instead, is Yengee. I kill him myself, someday. He hokay? Look dead, last time we see him."

"American, then?" Deriabin mused, ignoring Black Claw's question. "Americans are as big thieves as British. Where did you and this 'Luckydan' come from?"

"Canoe down big river, Lot of Water. Far up. What difference it make you, anyhow? Damn Gossacks don' own beavers, foxes, otters. Belong to selves, to land. Injuns want to catch 'em, trade with Gossacks or Hudson Bay men, that our business. Land don' belong to Gossacks or Hudson Bays or Bostons either. What I say."

Loon-cry laid a hand on Black Claw's arm, spoke quietly in Kutchin.

"I think we shouldn't tell this man anything, not until we see Danl-ock."

"Use English," the Russian said sharply. "No more secret talks. Who is this woman, Black Claw? Is she your wife, your daughter?"

Black Claw glanced at Loon-cry, shrugged, decided to let her bear her own witness.

She swallowed, spoke.

"I am Loon-cry, Danl-ock's woman. We married Whiteman's way. You must let Danl-ock come with wife, little-one-to-be. He don' steal nothin', don' want to hurt anybody. You let 'im out, we all go away."

"*Krahseeva*, very pretty," Deriabin nodded. "But that doesn't matter to me at all. Where did your husband trap those furs?"

Loon-cry looked at the Russian, let her face go blank.

"Don' know. Up there somewhere. Many rivers, many mountains between. Don' know how to say."

"*Yah pahnyeemahyoo*," the trader nodded. "I see. Who does he work for? It's Hudson's Bay, isn't it?"

"Don' know H.B.C. Danl-ock work for self, just like everybody."

"Remarkable. What do you know, Chief Black Claw? Do you have a better idea than Madame Loon-cry as to how you come to be here?"

Black Claw shrugged, grinned broadly.

"Nope. Me dumb Injun too."

When Dan awoke, the first thing he noticed was the throbbing in his head. When he began to take account of his surroundings, he found himself face down on a dirt floor in a hot, dark, foul-smelling place. As he lay still, hoping the thrumming pain would subside and the fog that seemed to wool his thought processes would clear, it occurred to him to wonder if perhaps he'd died, and further, if the fire-and-brimstone preachers of his youth had been right. Possibly he now found himself in some sort of anteroom of hell.

The place was no more than two paces in either direction and entirely windowless, although unchinked gaps between the logs of the structure admitted sufficient light for him to make out the features of the room. A wooden shelf was suspended from one wall, presumably to serve as a bed, and the sons of bitches had left him a single woolen blanket—nothing more, not even a slop bucket, he noted with disgust.

"Guess dead people don't need slop buckets, anyhow," he thought, although he'd already discarded his original thesis. "From the smell of this place, though, a honey pot might of been in order."

He got gingerly to his feet, staggered, lurched to a seat on the shelf. The fog in his brain was beginning to clear, and he remembered now the soldiers waving their weapons and his brief skirmish. Beyond that he remembered nothing until the present.

For several minutes he sat holding his head between his hands, pressing the palms against his temples as if to prevent an explosion.

They call you Lucky Danl-ock, not Smart. Ain't that the damn truth, Loon-gal? Why in hell did I try to take on three damn Russki soldiers? Lucky they didn't blow a hole in me. Lucky Danl-ock. What the hell did the Siberians do with Loon-cry? If the sons of bitches hurt her . . .

In all likelihood, he realized, they'd confined her and Black Claw elsewhere in the fort—either that or simply put them outside the palisades and told them to get lost, inasmuch as they were Indians. That in itself presented problems, though, for the Nulato Indians were probably cousins to the Koyukons and would thus consider all Kutchins as enemies. Still, it was not likely the devils would harm a woman, particularly a young, attractive, and obviously pregnant one. Getting her back from them, however, might be a different matter. If she were captured, almost certainly some warrior would claim her as a wife. And then there was the problem of Black Claw. . . .

The questions and anxieties rattled around like seeds in a gourd, and to distract himself Lucky Dan stood up, his legs less rubbery now, and pressed his eye to one of the larger spaces between logs. Brilliant afternoon sunlight glared off a yard of bare, packed earth where a few people went about the normal business of a small trading outpost. Two roughly-dressed *promyshlenniki* sat with their backs against the wall of a log building across the way, idly throwing knives at some target a few feet distant. A Koyukon woman carrying a bundle of laundry emerged from a doorway, doubtless taking it to a clear tributary river to wash—in exchange for a few beads or perhaps a bit of food for the two solemn, black-eyed children who trailed her. No one so much as glanced in his direction—and wouldn't have been able to see him if they had.

Dan moved now to the heavy door, tried it. As he'd expected, it didn't budge, almost certainly barred sturdily from the outside. Through a crack near the door he saw one of the soldiers who'd detained him—now lounging with his rifle slung over his shoulder and looking bored.

"Hey, you! You turd-eating Russki pighound!"

The guard glanced in his direction without sign of interest, turned away.

"Yeah, I mean you, you son of a bitch! Let me the hell out of here! They's laws against just lockin' a man up without even tellin' him what he done. You got any damn laws in Russia?"

The soldier looked his way again, shouted, "*Yah nyee pahnyeemahyoo.* Quiet, Angleeski!" Then he turned and began marching slowly back and forth, ignoring completely Dan's further outbursts.

After a time Locke tired of shouting and began pacing. He alternated his time between walking, yelling at the guard, who seemed to have become completely deaf, peering through one crack and another, and sitting on the hard wooden bed-shelf, brooding. Afternoon shadows grew longer and longer. Eventually a small opening appeared in the middle of the door, and a tin pan of wheat gruel with tiny chunks of gristly meat in it was shoved through. After that, nothing happened at all as the light eventually faded into long twilight, brief night, and twilight again.

Deriabin made no further headway in his attempt to extract information from Loon-cry and Black Claw, despite both promised riches in trade goods and various dire threats. Eventually, with an impatient gesture, he ordered the guards to put the two of them outside the palisade gate and bar the entryway.

At this point Lieutenant Bernard intervened.

"I'll take responsibility for these two, Deriabin, if you will allow it. They're welcome to stay in my quarters. You know how these tribes are—almost all of them are fighting with their neighbors. I understand your Nulato Koyukons are even at war with their kin living upstream. If you put the detainees at the mercy of the Nulatos, you could well be signing their death warrant. At least let the woman come to my quarters. She's with child, Vasily."

But Deriabin was in a temper and would not be moved.

"*Nyet!* No savages inside the post after dark. That is the rule."

"Hardly seems worth the bother, when the night's only an hour or so long. May I at least take the savages to my quarters and feed them, then? I'd like to interview them. Perhaps they've heard something of Sir John's expedition."

Deriabin looked on the verge of refusing this request as well, but then shrugged and laughed aloud.

"So far as I can tell, these two are deaf, dumb, and blind, but perhaps you will have better luck with them, my English friend. By all means—but they must be out of the post before ten o'clock. Is *official* nighttime. Rules are rules, Lieutenant."

In Bernard's quarters a round-faced, smiling Koyukon woman of perhaps forty served the three of them a meal of tasty caribou venison boiled with an assortment of wild roots and greens, these to be washed down with dark, sweet tea. While they ate, the naval officer explained his reason for being at Nulato—how the third and final expedition of the explorer Sir John Franklin had ended with shipwreck in pack ice in the Polar Sea. The remains of the vessels had been found, but Sir John and many of his crew had vanished, and presumably had departed over the ice. The captain of Bernard's ship, the *Enterprise*, had heard rumors when he put in at Redoubt St. Michael—of possible sightings of Whitemen in a tributary valley some miles upstream from Nulato. Captain Collison had procured permission for Bernard to accompany Deriabin, in St. Michael at the time, to Nulato to investigate the rumors.

"You've come down from upriver, you say. Have you heard anything of Whitemen upstream, perhaps in Koyukuk Valley?"

Black Claw shrugged.

"Only White devils I know about are Hudson Bays at fort by our village."

"And what fort would that be?" Bernard asked, smiling as he did so.

Loon-cry, unsure whether to trust this White man, whom she'd already decided to rename "Pretty Coat," laid a restraining hand on Black Claw's arm.

The Lieutenant saw the gesture, nodded, smiled again.

"You're right to be cautious, Miss . . . Madame. If the fort your friend speaks of is the one I suspect it is, it's better that our Russian host knows nothing about it. You're speaking, I imagine, of either Murray's post, Fort Youcan, or Campbell's Fort Selkirk. Probably the former. . . . What you say of it tells me that the Youcan and the Kuikpak are indeed the identical river. Is that so?"

Loon-cry searched the officer's face. His eyes were the same peculiar sky color as Danl-ock's, his hair only a slightly darker red-brown, and both faces were creased into friendly wrinkles around the mouth and eyes. On grounds which had nothing to do with reason but in which she had complete confidence, she decided she trusted this Hudson's Bay. She nodded.

"Is same river. But we don' hear nothing about any other Whitemen. Long way from ocean."

"Yes, well, we can't leave a stone unturned, however unlikely. How many days' travel did you come from Fort Youcan?"

As the talk went on, Lieutenant Bernard questioned the two closely on the lay of the land upstream, landmarks, directions, watersheds—and seemed to have forgotten about the shipwrecked men. Loon-cry noted this, but was not concerned with Pretty Coat's reasons, having more pressing concerns on her mind. At length, when the lieutenant seemed to have run out of questions, she leaned forward and spoke with urgent intensity.

"You will help Danl-ock, Pretty Coat? I am sorry, I forget your other name. See you have beautiful coat, color of sky, bright buttons like sun. . . ."

The young officer laughed almost bashfully, blushed beneath his tan.

"My name is John Bernard, Madame, but I am honored to be thought of as Pretty Coat. And I assure you that I'll do everything in my power to assist your husband, although I'm afraid I have very little influence with Vasily Deriabin at the moment. . . ."

"Is worthless Boston devil, hokay," Black Claw growled, "but still we want him back. Someday I pay off debt to Looncry, then I kill 'im."

"I say! Well, I certainly hope not. In any event, Mrs. . . . Locke, is it? I'll do anything I can. I wish I could offer you accommodation here, but Deriabin is unshakeable. It's villainous to throw out a young woman like you, particularly in your, ah, condition. . . ."

"I take care of her, Mist' Bernard."

It was Bernard's Koyukon serving-woman, silent until this moment, who had spoken. She stepped forward now, still smiling broadly, and touched at Loon-cry's smooth hair.

"Oh, that's splendid, Salmon Berry," Bernard cried. "You'll be in very good hands with Salmon Berry, I assure you," he added, turning to Loon-cry again. "Her brother is one of the elders, very influential in the tribe."

"Is true," Salmon Berry nodded. "Nobody bother you if I say so."

"You are kind," Loon-cry said, rising, "but my friend. . . . "

Her eyes turned to Black Claw.

"You don' wan' leave this one, even though he got big scar on face?" the older woman laughed, then winked broadly at Black Claw, who quickly looked away, jaw set.

"He pretty ugly, all right," Salmon Berry continued, "but he come too, you want."

"Don' need no help from womans, by God," Black Claw grumbled. "I sleep by gate, come in morning to check on Luckydan."

"You must come, Black Claw," Loon-cry said. "I saved your life, not Danl-ock."

"I just foolin', anyhow," Salmon Berry said, giving Black Claw another wide grin. "Be nice to have man in lodge again, even bad-natured Kutchin. You come."

Black Claw held out a moment longer, then shrugged.

"I come, hokay. Maybe save Loon-cry's life from blood-thirsty Koyukons, then we even. But don' you go gettin' ideas, old woman. I got one wife already, sometimes she's more than I want."

Despite Lieutenant Bernard's best efforts in his behalf, Lucky Dan remained in the odious post jail for what seemed like an eternity. After a few days, he was no longer confined to the little building twenty-four hours a day, but was let out occasionally to exercise on the grounds, under guard. This privilege, however, as well as his meals, seemed to be ruled by whim or by someone happening to remember his existence, for there were days that passed during which he saw no one at all, and the long, daylight period of sweltering semigloom in his confines would pass into brief darkness and back out before the little slot in the door would open and a plate of very poor food would come through. During such long periods of enforced isolation, he sometimes had reason to fear for his sanity.

At these times he entertained himself by singing every bawdy-house song he could recall, or by counting the marks he'd carefully scratched upon the wall to number the days of his imprisonment, although as time passed he became less and less certain that he had not forgotten to mark some days or had noted others more than once. Then the attempt to remember and his inability to be sure became like an intolerable mental itch, and he again felt himself poised on the edge of madness.

"Ain't like I never been alone in my life before," he counseled himself, forcing the matter of the day-marks out of his head. "Hell, I've gone months sometimes without seein' another human critter, and it never bothered me a bit. Well, it never bothered me a whole lot, anyhow."

But that was different, an' ye know it.

Different to be moving, one eye out for hostile Indians or grizzly bear, the other watching the weather and the signs of animal passage. Different to be breathing air without bounds, feeling the sun on his back or the misery of days of soaking rain, or seeing the world turned to burning cold and achingly beautiful crystal white in winter moonlight or the ghosts of fog.

Different to look off across a perfectly God-and-man-for-saken little lake and see a bald-headed eagle hit the water, a fountain of spray, and the big bird instantly veer up and wing heavily away, wriggling silver flashing in its talons. Different to stalk a bull moose to the edge of an overgrown marsh just for the hell of it—just to watch the shaggy brown beast standing knee deep in coarse grass with a thatch of green hanging from its jaws and a perfectly blank, perfectly happy expression on its foolish, flop-nosed face.

Different to be free, damn it. He'd never once been lonely when he was free.

He had numerous interviews with Deriabin, interviews in which the suspicious Russian-American Company factor would try by various means to extract information from him concerning how he came to be where he was, where he came from, and how he happened to be in possession of H.B.C. goods. After a few of these, Dan began to amuse himself by telling Deriabin a different story each time he was asked the inevitable questions, driving the Russian agent to fits of red-faced rage and horrendous threats which never materialized.

After a time, however, the two developed a grudging admiration for one another, and when the questions had been asked and answered mostly as a matter of form, Vasily Deriabin and Lucky Dan would digress into story-swapping sessions.

As for Lieutenant Bernard, who was also allowed to visit him a few times, he was less sure. The British officer told him each time that he was continuing to do everything he could think of to procure Dan's freedom, that at the very worst Locke would have to remain in the jail only until Bernard's own departure, for he'd procured Deriabin's promise that the American trapper could leave on Bernard's boat with him, so long as Locke agreed never to set foot in Russian Alaska again.

But Dan suspected that there was a good deal the lieutenant was not telling him. He found it impossible to believe the story that Bernard was searching for possible shipwreck survivors some two hundred miles from the coast and several hundred miles from the site of the disaster. Further, it was difficult to believe that the Russians, always suspicious if nothing else, were buying such a story and providing assistance in the British effort.

Some sort of secret deal being cooked up between the Brits and the Russkies, something neither would want Americans to get wind of?

In truth, however, such matters interested Lucky Dan very little. The North Country was so damned big and so easy to get lost in that, as far as he could see, it made very little difference who had nominal political claim to it.

The bare facts, Dan eventually admitted to himself, were that he would probably like Bernard quite well if the son of a bitch didn't spend so much time singing the praises of Loon-cry. The poor sot was obviously smitten with her, and, what was worse, too damned *civilized* to admit it even to himself.

Loon-cry. Might as well face up to it. The worst part of the whole stinking mess was being separated from her.

It was also true, however, that the only thing making his isolation bearable was that, almost every day at some time during the day, he could look out through one chink in the wall or another and see her standing somewhere about the grounds, in sight but kept from communicating with him by watchful guards.

On occasion she slipped past one who was looking the other way and whispered to him through the cracks, crying, promising him he'd be out soon, and passing along such post gossip or rumor as she had.

Most of this news, except for reports on the activity of the unborn child, its vigorous kicking and what Loon-cry was sure were its dream-communications with her, concerned Black Claw and that old bastard's new love.

"Salmon Berry, she got eyes for Black Claw," she would say at one time, "but he pretend he won' have nothin' to do with her. He just bluffing, though."

Another time she reported, "Black Claw softenin' up, all right. Not much longer, now, those two." Then added, pretending to be angry, "You better not try bringin' in second wife on me some time. I take your little horn an' hang him round my neck."

But when the marks on the wall numbered thirty-three, by Dan's best count, several days passed and Loon-cry didn't show up in the yard. Those were very black days for Dan, and neither Deriabin nor Bernard came to enlighten him as to her condition. During that interval he scratched five marks on the wall—although on his best, if unreliable, recall, only three days passed.

Then, on the morning of the third or the fourth or the fifth day, the big door was unbarred, and standing before him was not only Deriabin but Lieutenant Bernard and Black Claw as well.

"*Dah, dah*, you come with us, Daniel Locke," Deriabin said, looking his sternest and most sour. "*Skahryehyee!* Don't stand there! Come!"

Locke blinked in the sudden brilliant sunlight.

"Loon-cry?" he demanded, unable to ask more.

"Never mind Loon-cry," the Russian growled, but Lucky Dan saw that Bernard was looking utterly sappy—and Black Claw was having a hard time concealing a broad grin.

"Just come with us, worthless Boston sombitch," the one-eyed Kutchin said, and then he and Bernard were both pounding Lucky Dan on the back.

"*Skahryehyee!*" the Russian repeated, cracking a grin.

Dan followed them across the packed yard, and then Bernard stepped forward and flung open a door with a flourish. Lucky Dan suddenly felt unable to move, although by now he'd pretty well figured out what was up. Black Claw and Deriabin pushed him forward, however, and then stepped back as he entered the room.

At first he could see little in the dimness after the bright yard, but then a thin wailing focused his attention. He moved toward it, saw a round-faced Indian woman standing beside a bed, grinning from ear to ear, and he looked down.

Loon-cry lay against pillows. Her face was tired, but she smiled and her eyes glowed in the faint light. He knelt beside her, feeling utterly confused, awed, and a little frightened, kissed her, brushed at her hair, kissed her again.

"Foolish White-devil," she whispered, and then from somewhere produced a small bundle in layers of leather wrappings.

Yes, that's what it is, that's where the noise is coming from. Baby. Sweet, black-feathered, pointy-beaked Jesus-Gawd. The baby!

"You not wish to hold daughter, Danl-ock?"

7

Winter Massacre

Either the advent of Lucky Dan Locke's fatherhood touched some secret chord of sympathy in Vasily Deriabin, or he had decided that a full month's imprisonment was sufficient for the *Amerikan* interloper. Whatever the case, from the time Locke stepped forth from the miserable post jail to view his daughter, he had been a free man, and furthermore, the Russian-American Company agent now seemed intent upon adopting Lucky Dan and his small family. On the night of the birth, he insisted that the new father drink toast after toast with him, until both men were staggering and singing, alternately, sad Russian peasant songs and American alehouse favorites. He produced from some private store of keepsakes a small silver crucifix and chain, which he presented as a gift to the newborn a few days later, when mother and child were up to receiving visitors.

"Maybe ye shouldn't be giving this away," Dan said, turning the exquisitely ornamented cross over and seeing an inscription in tiny Cyrillic characters on the back. "Must of belonged to your mother or grandmother or some such."

"*Pahzháloosta*, please, is only small gift. It pleasures me much more for little one to have it than for me to keep it locked away in box."

"We are honored by gift from Gossack chief," Loon-cry said quickly. "We tell our daughter of the one who gave it, and she will treasure this beautiful thing."

Deriabin mumbled a few awkward words and backed out of the room.

"Wonder what the old Russki fox is up to," Dan muttered. "Keeps me locked up in a damned airless hole for a month,

75

doesn't even remember to feed me half the time, and now he's my best friend. Don't add up."

"Is not bad man, Danl-ock," Loon-cry said, smiling as she put her finger into the baby's tiny hand to grasp. "He thought you were enemy, now thinks you not. You not see he is man who had child, children some time? Something sad must have happen to them, or else his own little one have pretty necklace. You not see tears in Gossack's eyes when he look at our daughter? Is not bad man."

Loon-cry seemed fully content with her explanation of things, but Dan chose to reserve judgment for the time being.

For his part, Black Claw was as proprietary of the infant girl as if he had created her himself. On the fourth day of her life, he insisted on presiding over a naming ceremony.

"Sure, fair enough, I guess," Lucky Dan agreed. "We're callin' her Naomi, after my grandmother. Loon-cry says that's all right with her."

"Is good name, name from father's ancestor," Loon-cry nodded, crooning softly to the infant who smiled blankly into space.

"No, by damn!" Black Claw exploded. "Not givin' worthless Boston name to my granddaughter."

"Your granddaughter, ye old scoundrel! Where do ye get off with that?"

"Loon-cry my daughter by marriage, hokay, baby is my granddaughter. Stupid Whiteman don't understand nothing."

Eventually a compromise was reached, and the next morning the tiny girl was introduced to the rising sun, the river, and the four directions as Naomi Walks-Between-Worlds, the first in grudging deference to Lucky Dan, and the second part of the name that which had occurred to Salmon Berry in a vision. It was, in fact, the round-faced Koyukon widow who convinced Black Claw of the propriety of Dan's contribution.

"Is right she have Whitewoman's name, because in my dream I saw that she will walk in Whiteman's world as well as this world we know. That is why we give her other name, Walks-Between-Worlds."

Lieutenant Bernard left the post a few days later on an expedition upriver, ostensibly to question whatever tribes he found concerning possible whereabouts of the shipwrecked men. As he expected the trip to last for some months, he pressed Lucky Dan and Loon-cry to make use of his quarters while he was gone, Deriabin apparently willing, now, to make an exception to his rule concerning Indians inside the fort. Salmon Berry seemed quite pleased with the prospect of having Black Claw to herself.

"People gonna talk, gonna think we married, now, just the two of us livin' there," the widow giggled.

"Just you remember what I say, Woman, don' get no big idea," Black Claw scowled. "Soon as I get Luckydan killed, I go back home. Already got one wife too many, hokay."

"Maybe I do her little favor, though, later tonight," he added, breaking into a grin and winking at Dan.

"Ho! Maybe I do you *big* favor," Salmon Berry laughed. "Just like last night. Who say I want you to stay, anyhow? Ugly as wart on toad's backside, mean as grizzly bear with sour berries in his gut. Maybe I just play with you until real man comes along."

"Real man! I show you real man," Black Claw roared, clutching at his groin and charging toward the woman.

"You hush now," Loon-cry scolded. "Waking up baby. Such a way for her grandfather to act."

Salmon Berry shrieked in mock fear and then ran heavily out of Dan and Loon-cry's quarters, giggling as Black Claw pursued her.

"The ol' Claw has gone downright kittenish on us," Dan laughed.

"Is in love, I guess. You gonna fall in love with other woman when we old like Black Claw?"

"Never, Loon-darlin'. But I might take in a couple of Nulato virgins to tide me over till we can play games again."

"Long time. Have to wait until baby is weaned. . . . "

Dan glanced over at the little creature, sleeping peacefully in a packing crate provided by Deriabin. The perfect pink mouth moved in sleep as if nursing, and Lucky Dan felt his insides squeeze with pure love.

"Maybe my luck-medicine'll work, an' she'll grow her some teeth in a month or so an' start chawing on meat. . . . "

"Is maybe one little favor I do for you," Loon-cry smiled, moving to the front door and bolting it. Then she took Dan's hand and drew him into the curtained-off bedroom. "Is only fair I get to nurse on something, too," she added with a gleam in her eye as she unbuttoned his trousers. "You not believe so, Lucky Dan?"

Then her lips were upon him, and he could not think of a thing to say.

Deriabin's newfound generosity toward Locke did not extend itself so far as the matter of the pelts Lucky Dan had brought in. No amount of talking could persuade the agent either to return them or to pay the trapper their value.

"*Prahsteetyee*, my friend, but furs trapped on Russian land, they belong to Company already. Why we pay for them? You are lucky man, free from jail even though you stole these furs. If you want to go to work, I pay you what I pay top trapper."

"But why the hell won't ye pay me that much for the pelts I already trapped for ye?"

"Is different. Those were stolen."

"Right. Ye stole 'em from me."

"I am sorry, Lucky Dan. I like you, you got nice family. But the Russian-American company will not pay thief to return property. Is company policy. Sit down, now, have nice glass of tea with me."

Locke stalked out of the office without another word and returned to Loon-cry, who was nursing Naomi. She watched quietly as he stormed around the room, cursing the Russian agent soundly. When he at last calmed down, he sat on the bed beside her.

"Looks like we're goin' to be stayin' right here for a spell. Without the skins the damned Russki thief took, we ain't got any money to catch a boat south."

"Is okay. I like it here just fine, Danl-ock. Got you, got Naomi Walks-Between-Worlds, got Black Claw and Salmon Berry for friends."

"That's good, because we're gonna be spendin' the winter here. I've got to trap back what we lost an' then some, and the pelts won't even be any good for another two, three months."

Loon-cry nodded, smiled down at the baby, who had fallen asleep nursing and now lay, head turned away from the breast, eyes closed and a dribble of milk still hanging in the corner of the rosebud mouth.

"Ye sure that kid ain't weaned yet? Looks to me like she's gettin' a set of teeth on 'er that'd tear the hide off a bull moose."

"Silly Danl-ock. Bostons got no patience, just like Black Claw says."

In the strange flux of her new motherhood, the summer drifted almost as a dream to Loon-cry, time seeming to pass both very quickly and not at all, so that each moment she spent with the warm little creature pressed against her body and pulling at her breast, each interval of gazing into the intent baby face or stroking the round head seemed a perfect, complete eternity, and yet the days followed after one another with almost alarming rapidity, and each day, it seemed to her, the infant was changing, growing so fast that Loon-cry was almost fearful Naomi would grow out of her arms and into a young woman, would be shyly flirting with some young man, and then be a mother of her own babies before Loon-cry even had time to comprehend her infancy.

Long, golden days of the brief Northern summer followed one another with their short intervals of darkness, but even now, in the warmth of summer, the periods of night grew noticeably longer. Danl-ock was gone a good deal, he and Black Claw kept busy with hunting to provide meat for the long winter ahead. The relatively brief times when he was home were especially happy for Loon-cry. The husband and wife would often go for aimless walks along the river or back into the hills away from it, taking turns at carrying Naomi in her cradleboard and talking. She would often ask him to tell her again about the strange lands to the south where they would go in the spring, the rivers that never froze and the places where snow almost never fell. She tried to envision these places, and would make him repeat the details over and over so that she could remember and think about them during the times when he was gone. And when they were tired, they would sleep wrapped in each other's arms.

During periods while Danl-ock was off hunting with Black Claw, Loon-cry spent much of her time visiting with Salmon Berry and sometimes with her pregnant daughter-in-law as well, Snow Flower. Loon-cry usually slept with Naomi in the Koyukon woman's cozy lodge rather than returning to the trad-

ing post at night, although Bernard was still gone on his upriver
venture and his quarters were empty.

In the older woman's gossip, advice, good-natured grum-
bling, and obvious affection for both Naomi and herself, Loon-
cry discovered a friendship that corresponded to a deep need,
something perhaps, as she sometimes thought, like the rela-
tionship she might have had with the mother she had never
known.

"You know, you shouldn't pick that baby up ever' time
she cry a little bit," Salmon Berry would advise frequently.
"Make her fussy, bad, she know she gonna get her way whenever she holler."

But always, the next time Naomi began to whimper, Salmon
Berry would run to her, unlace her from the cradleboard, and
rock her in her arms, crooning nonsense songs until the baby
fell quiet again.

Once, Loon-cry said, "I think maybe you only tell me not
to pick up Naomi so you can do it. Well, soon Snow Flower's
child will come, and then you'll have two of them to spoil."

Salmon Berry laughed, gently tickled the little one's nose.

"No, is true what I say. Is what my mother told me. I got
good sense, but soft heart. Never listen to good sense part."

Another time, as the two women worked side by side,
scraping caribou hides while the meat from Black Claw and
Danl-ock's most recent hunting venture dried on a rack nearby,
Salmon Berry said, with no lead-in, "That Boston man better
treat you and little one good, or I kill him if Black Claw don't."

"Why you say that?" Loon-cry asked, surprised. "Danl-
ock loves us. He always good to us."

"Seems like good man, hokay. Just that many times, Koyukon woman go with Gossack man, have his children, then
one day he just leave, she alone with little ones to raise, no
man to help. Very hard for her then, if she don't have family."

"Danl-ock would never do that. He is best man I know."

"You probably right, nothin' to worry. Just if, well, you
ever need help, need family, you come stay with me. I raised
three sons, two still alive, but never had no daughter. Always
wanted a girl to keep me company. That why I love you an'
Snow Flower too. Like her better than worthless son, in fact."

Loon-cry looked up, too moved to speak, feeling tears
starting to her eyes. Salmon Berry grinned at her, moved a

hand as if to brush away thanks or even the suggestion that what she'd said was significant in any way, then briefly squeezed Loon-cry's hand.

"I found a mother at the same time I became one. I am very lucky woman," Loon-cry whispered.

The long days shortened rapidly, and in only two moons from the time of Naomi's birth the year reached the point of balance, the period of daylight equaling the period of darkness, but always the days growing shorter. As the time of light grew shorter and the warmth went out of the earth, Lucky Dan returned from his last hunting trip for the fall season and spent a month at the fort with Loon-cry and Naomi. Lieutenant Bernard returned from his own upstream venture, but gallantly volunteered to stay in the Company barracks with the crew of the fort, leaving Loon-cry and Lucky Dan in private possession of his quarters. Lucky Dan passed his time cleaning and oiling his traps, making snowshoes, repairing sleds that belonged to the Company, and performing various other tasks necessary for preparation for the winter's trapping.

At other times he played with the baby, whose growth always astounded him when he returned from a few days' absence, and frequently he and Loon-cry and the baby would visit with Black Claw and Salmon Berry, who seemed to be getting along like thieves.

The time passed happily and all too quickly. The days grew short and the first snows fell, while between storms, with the sun showing above the horizon for only a few hours bracketing noon and the nights brilliant with the cold, coruscating fire of the aurora blazed across heaven, and temperatures dropped below the zero mark on the thermometer and stayed there.

In a matter of days, ice formed along the edges of the great river, then reached out to join in a crust across the stream, and finally froze into a solid layer to a depth of several inches, firm enough to support an army and more than solid enough to allow travel by dogsled. It was this event that Locke and the other trappers had been awaiting. Lucky Dan and Black Claw made preparations for departure the following day.

Loon-cry hung about close to Lucky Dan as he packed the dogsled in darkness. The cold was intense, the night utterly clear, and the sky awash with stars. To the north great sheets of iridescent green and blue-white played across heaven. Frost glittered in Locke's beard from the instant condensation and freezing of his breath, and when Loon-cry spoke, her voice was muffled by the ruff of her parka, which was pulled up over her mouth and nose so that only a circle around her eyes showed.

"You be gone a long time, Danl-ock?" she asked.

"Couple of months if we have a good hunt, maybe longer if pickings are slim and we have to move further out."

"Is very long time."

The muffled voice sounded so sad that Dan paused in his packing, embraced her clumsily through the thick layers of their clothing.

"Hell, I'll be back pesterin' you so soon, ye'll wish I'd of stayed away longer. Ye'll likely have young Looie Bernard dancin' attendance on ye while I'm gone. Maybe I should shoot the son of a bitch before I go. . . . "

"Don' talk silly, Danl-ock. I'm afraid. . . . "

"Ye ain't afraid of grizzly bears, gal. Ye're just tryin' to fool me into thinkin' ye'll miss me. Help me with that lashing there, will you?"

Loon-cry complied and kept silent until the two returned to the welcome warmth of their quarters, a good fire blazing in the mud hearth. Then she shrugged out of her outer layers of clothing, and the two sat on a bearskin in front of the fire, arms about each other, until Naomi Walks-Between-Worlds cried and Loon-cry rose to nurse her. When the baby, satiated and asleep, had been put back into her cradle, Loon-cry returned to Dan and slowly began removing his clothing.

"Baby is weaned now," she whispered.

"That a fact? She don't *look* weaned. . . . "

"Is weaned until next time she get hungry. Then maybe she stop being weaned, I don' know. I want to do something so you will remember me all those months you be gone. . . . "

"Sounds good to me. Ye sure ye ain't going to upset the seasons, cause the volcanoes to go off, somethin' like that?"

"Silly. Is not rule, just what people do. This time is different, is—what that word? Means you got to do something quick?"

"An emergency?"

"Yes. Is emergency. Kiss me, Danl-ock. Will be long time. You think you remember Loon-cry?"

Then she stood, slipped her elkskin dress off over her head, stepped out of the leggings and the red flannel underwear she wore beneath. Firelight gleamed and danced on long lines and curves of hip, shoulder, swollen, brown-nippled breasts. Dan sucked in a quick breath at her beauty, something that always seemed to surprise him, and then she was beside him, kissing, fondling, caressing him until his manhood stood rigid. She drew in a breath, then, and straddled him, let herself down with a long sigh, moved slowly up and down, head back, black hair like a storm over her shoulders.

Dan groaned, and then with a great effort of will grasped her hips and gently lifted her off, pulled her to him and kissed her, ran his hands over her body, down over breasts and rounded belly, up the insides of her thighs and then to the soft center, until her breaths came in quick gasps and her hips moved. She moaned and tossed, her body tightening until she convulsed with a long cry.

He mounted her then, moving slowly, holding himself back as she continued to gasp, hips thrusting blindly, and then he could hold back no longer, flesh moving against flesh in quickening rhythm, mounting unbearably until he groaned aloud, and the pure peace of release took him and he drifted, mindless, down into feathery darkness. As he lay on the very edge of unconsciousness, he heard her voice, as if from a great distance.

"You remember Loon-cry now, Danl-ock?"

"I'll try, damn me if I won't try," he muttered, drawing her down in his arms and letting himself slip completely into the pleasant abyss.

In the morning hours before the late winter sunrise, Lucky Dan set off in company with Black Claw and a crew of half a dozen post trappers of Koyukon, Aleut, and Russian-Indian Creole heritage, men who would move off on their own, in pairs, at various points upriver. Loon-cry watched the dark figures of men and dogs, dimly delineated against Kuikpak ice and snow in the starlight, until they had vanished, although the clamor of the dogs still returned through the distance. Then she walked back to the post and nursed Naomi, feeling a great sense of emptiness inside and trying not to ask herself and the dark that pressed against the one small four-paned window the question:

Will I ever see Danl-ock again? Will he bother to come back to us?

She moved out of Lieutenant Bernard's quarters and into Salmon Berry's lodge, although the naval officer pressed her to remain, assuring her that he was quite happy in the barracks. She thanked him for his kindness but would not be moved from her plan. She was, in fact, much more comfortable with the widow in Nulato village. Life there was, she had discovered, different only in minor details from life in her own village, and although she'd grown more or less accustomed to the ways of Whitemen in their outposts, she did not feel entirely easy living among them with Danl-ock absent.

In Salmon Berry's kashim she kept herself occupied with the tasks that were familiar and comforting to her. She sewed clothes for herself and the baby and Danl-ock against his return, chewed hides to soften them, helped Salmon Berry to prepare meals for her sons and brothers when they came to visit, and, along with Salmon Berry, presided at the birth of Snow Flower's daughter.

With Bernard's return to his solitary quarters, he requested Salmon Berry to resume her chores for him, and frequently Loon-cry accompanied the older woman to assist her and keep her company.

Both Bernard and Deriabin continued to be very solicitous toward the young mother and child, asking after the health of both until it nearly drove her mad, one or the other inviting her to dinner several times a week, and, when she declined, sending hot food over for her even though Black Claw and Danl-ock had provided more than enough meat to get the women and child through the winter. Further, in the forced inactivity of winter in the post, Lieutenant Bernard took to carving toys for the baby, bringing little boats and dolls and whistles over, always taking his hat off in Loon-cry's presence and blushing like a young boy when she praised his handiwork. She knew his obvious infatuation with her annoyed Danl-ock, but she found it rather endearing, particularly as he never made the slightest advance toward her.

The days of her husband's absence, then, passed with a soothing monotony, and she kept careful track, beginning to anticipate his possible return when two cycles of the moon had passed. By that time the period of ascendency of darkness had passed, and the period of daylight began to grow perceptibly longer, although very little. Storms of snow and wind continued to sweep up the Lot-of-Water and rage about them for a few days, and other times the skies cleared and temperatures plummeted. Winter still had the northlands very much in its grip, and pale fires still danced in the dark skies.

But Danl-ock did not return, and Loon-cry grew visibly restless. Even though he'd told her that he could well be gone for more than two months and indeed possibly until the time of ice-breaking on the river, the end of that period marked the beginning of the time when she began to expect him, and she could not stop herself from going frequently to the river on some excuse or another, walking out onto the ice, and straining her vision into the distance.

"He come back to you, don't worry," Salmon Berry said one day. "You right first time. Luckydan loves you."

"Sure, he come back. I know that." Loon-cry nodded. Then she turned to Salmon Berry, her eyes wide with worry. "You really think so? Has been gone so long. . . . "

"Not so long. Only long to you because you so young . . . and because you are in love. Good thing Salmon Berry old enough to know better."

"Know better than what?"

"Know better than be in love. Me an' Black Claw, we both too old for such silliness. We know enough just have fun with each other. Someday he go back to his village, I stay here."

"I don' believe what you say. You miss him, too."

"Well, maybe I miss him little bit. . . . "

The moon grew from thin crescent, hanging in the western sky when the sun went down, through fingernail curve, through fat oval, to a full silver globe lighting the earth through the long darkness, shrank back to a thin crescent hanging in the eastern sky before dawn—and still the trapping party had not returned. Now the time had come when the periods of daylight were gaining rapidly on the darkness. More snows fell, but the season was now clearly pulling toward the time when darkness and light should equal one another.

Loon-cry slept fitfully, waking often from dreams of terror that she couldn't remember clearly, although the fear was distinct and remained with her as she struggled to return to sleep. Through the darkness she heard what sounded like a strangled scream, the sound cut off so abruptly that she was left wondering whether it had truly occurred.

Then she detected vague sounds of movement, something that didn't belong in the village at night. She slipped from her robes, stepped to Salmon Berry's pallet. The older woman slept undisturbed, and Loon-cry was just leaning down to waken her when the lodge suddenly sprang to light.

She cried out even before she turned, saw the fearfully painted figure of a man, short-bodied and powerful-looking, pine torch in one hand and war club in the other. When he saw her, the red paint around his mouth split around stained teeth as he grinned at her. In a moment two more warriors crowded through the entryway. Out of the corner of her eye, Loon-cry saw that Salmon Berry was sitting up, her robes still clutched around her—suddenly beginning to scold at the men as if she knew them.

And then everything suddenly slowed down. The first warrior raised his club and struck the woman. Blood appeared on her temple, and she dropped instantly.

"Salmon Berry!" Loon-cry gasped, and then a muscular arm was around her waist, dragging her after him.

"My baby!" she screamed, struggling instinctively to pull free, groping toward the blankets where Naomi still slept.

Then, simultaneously, she heard the infant begin to wail and felt a crushing pressure against her skull. She felt her legs turn soft, her body losing control. She struggled desperately against loss of strength and a blackness that seemed to creep at the edges of her vision and spread inward. Light drew to a point, and then there was nothing.

8

Upriver Quest

Winter trapping had gone well indeed, and six full packs of plew were bound and sitting side by side and, of course, frozen as hard as though they were pallets of brick.

Ice fogs swirled about the encampment, and during those intervals of forty and fifty below, Lucky Dan and Black Claw remained within their big thatched shelter that looked like nothing so much as an oversized wood-rat den—or, rather, almost like an igloo except that it was relatively pointed at the top and had a few spruce boughs sticking randomly out of its coating of accumulated hoar frost, and of course had been constructed with a smoke hole at its center.

At other times, when temperatures rose to near zero, the two men were out and about, nearly engulfed in their hooded clothing, and the vapor of their breath freezing in the air before them as the sled dogs strained in harness over the courses of their traplines.

Beyond dividing the days into those when it was possible to be out and about and those when it was not, the men did not think in terms of degrees of temperature as they passed the shadowy season—working or sitting across from one another in their shelter, petting a favored dog or two, sometimes exchanging stories, sometimes going for hours without speaking at all, sometimes playing the hand game or using Dan's creased and battered deck of cards to compete at poker or twenty-one, using for chips stacks of thumbnail-sized spruce rounds they had carved for the purpose.

At times the aurora borealis described shifting rivers of light across the sky, often pale bands of silver-green, sometimes yellow or even pale crimson, so that the appearance was that of fire in the sky.

"By Gawd," Dan said, "I swear I'll never get used to it. When I was a boy in Missouri, I remember the aurora—but only once or twice. 'Northern lights,' that's what my daddy called them. But here in the land of the Lot of Water, why she's a whole different thing. Something crazy up there in the sky, I guess—whatever causes it."

"Ancient Ones," Black Claw said. "They walking one side of sky to other. Restless, I guess. Me, I'm restless too. Miss Salmon Berry. Damn good woman, hokay. Miss old Kutchin wife too—Little Redpoll. She old and fat now, like me, but she pretty as Loon-cry once. I got picture in my mind—still looks like that, even though I know she don't. Funny about how time passes. Every year everything young again except people. All time we gettin' old an' dying—ain't that so? Used to wrestle grizzly bears for fun—then got my eye tore open, someabitch bear. . . ."

"Loon-cry," Dan mused, "and little Naomi. She's eight months now, going on nine. Be walking and talking soon— hell, maybe she already is. Gawddamn it, here I got the prettiest wife in the whole Youcan and a young one to boot—and I spend my time wandering around through the taiga, trapping and shooting varmints and afterward sitting in a hut with you. No offense, you understand, Mighty Warrior, but I'd prefer to be sharing quarters with Loon-cry. For one thing, I don't have to worry about my wife sticking a knife between my ribs. For another thing. . . ."

Black Claw spat into the air.

"Lodge always stinks when little ones come. Kids always messing, gotta keep changing 'em. Stink dirty. Bostons do that, or make their women do it, huh? Well, you don' got to worry for little while yet, Luckydan. Can't kill you yet. Raven's Egg go kinda crazy, beatin' on Loon-cry. Guess I don't like that. Other thing—maybe you ought to go find black sow bear curled up in a cave. Probably bear don't mind if you pull down your breeches an' poke her little. Jus' don't try crawling under my robes, hokay?"

Dan laughed as he stared up at the shifting patterns of light in the sky.

"Never fear, you cranky old bastard. You're safe—not my type."

"Can't even play hand game right," Black Claw said as he

turned and trudged back toward the hut and the fire inside and the pot of beaver tail and caribou tongue that was surely boiling by now.

Eventually, however, the gray-white lock of winter was broken, not all at once, but by slow degrees—with temperatures rising gradually, so that one morning Lucky Dan and Black Claw made note that no hoar frost had formed on the boughs and boles of spruce trees that night, and, indeed, the ice on shallow ponds had begun to go rotten and slushy blue in places.

The sled dogs, freed from their harness now, were off on a three-day jaunt, perhaps keeping company with some local wolves. Elk were bugling back among the forest fastnesses of the Kuskowim Mountains, and a month past the time of equal light and dark, the upper reaches of Nowitna River were running free of ice. A soft, warm rain had set in, and in the trackless forest animal activity was everywhere in evidence—both black bears and shaggy grizzlies were out and about, eating large quantities of early vegetation and tearing up downfall logs to get at termites, carpenter ants, and white wood grubs within. Wolves and coyotes were singing at night, their quavering notes echoing from canyon wall to canyon wall, and the sled dogs answering in kind as best they could. And birds. Red-throated loons and mudhens and ouzels and camp-robber jays and golden-beaked puffins. Birds everywhere.

With the trapping season essentially over, the two men set to work constructing rafts of poles and caribou hide—something sufficient to transport their highly successful season's take of plew and their dogs and sleds as well down the Nowitna to the Youcan and so on to Nulato.

"Goddam rich men now," Black Claw mumbled as he stretched and fastened sections of hide into place. "Deriabin, he don't steal what we got this time. I buy new steel knife, one with long, sharp blade. You tell me about Injuns on Miz-you-ri River, *scalp* Goddam Bostons. You show me how they do that, hokay, Luckydan?"

Black Claw winked his bad eye—a behavior trait Locke had always found somewhat unnerving.

"Hell yes," Dan replied, pulling at his chin whiskers, "be happy to demonstrate. You'll look good with a little red cap on top of your head. Of course, when a man gets scalped, his face sort of sags out of shape all around. Just what I've been told, is all. Never actually saw such a thing myself."

Black Claw paid no attention to the remarks as he worked deftly with a bone awl and a length of rawhide lacing.

"Hope Salmon Berry ain't found some other good-lookin' fella," he said at last.

It was Easter season as the linked rafts laden with men and dogs and equipment and bales of furs made their way two hundred miles along the Nowitna to the Kuikpak and onward down the great river, whose silt-laden current was still encumbered with drifting ice in places, nearly another two hundred miles to Nulato. A time of rebirth—all the more remarkable in the Far North after the fierce cold and darkness of winter, as suddenly the dormant earth, its permafrost thawing back sufficiently to allow plant growth, gave in to the urgings of life—life, indeed, that seemed a virtual explosion, side by side in places with lingering snowdrifts. Cottonwoods and alders along the river were in new leaf, and tangles of willow brush were studded with catkins. Mallards and loons and mudhens started up from the turbid water, and kingfishers darted along above the current, their repeated cries seemingly reflective of ancient avian antagonisms.

Dan thought of rebirth as they moved along—how everything in nature conspired with the Christian observance of death-into-life in reflection of deep energies now set loose by the warmth of lengthening days—energies not at all quieted by frequent heavy chill of morning fogs or by incoming rain storms. The whole business, he reflected, was some sort of grand contest between Raven Man and Jesus—if, indeed, Jesus was the one who caused something down within the cold tangles of roots to begin to move, the seeds to burst into upward-seeking shoots. Or was it Jesus who hid in the hard frost down underneath, fighting a losing battle this time of year against the forces of life?

Or perhaps the two entities were one and the same.

Locke was not a religious man, not in the usual sense of the word—rather a worshiper of the elemental forces of nature. Simple observation of these, without question, made more sense than pondering the obscure meanings recorded in what the Indians sometimes referred to as *White devil's medicine book.*

In any case, he mused, at the present moment the forces of life were moving toward the ascendant—glad, confident, and looking forward to whatever the brief but intense summer might bring. This time of year everything that had survived winter had its lungs full of something wonderful—something that, in the long run, couldn't be beaten.

During the times of fifty below, though, that was a different matter. . . .

"Bet that kid of mine, she's walking and reading Shakespeare by now," he called to Black Claw.

"White devil talk crazy, like always," Black Claw replied. "When we get back, me, I gonna jump in the blankets with Salmon Berry, get warm for once in life, hokay."

Lucky Dan threw back his head and laughed in pure happy anticipation.

He and Black Claw continued down the river, both men eager to reach Nulato. But what they discovered upon arriving at their destination hit Dan like a terrible fist driven to the pit of his stomach.

"Something wrong," Black Claw said as the dogs leaped into the water to swim the last few feet to shore, his voice almost a whisper.

Ambush, Dan's mind cautioned him. *Could be Koyukons hidden behind every damned gun slot. . . . What happened, could have happened? Nulato Indians went on a rampage? Loon-cry, God, Loon-cry. . . .*

The great gate of the palisade hung wide open, and as they passed through still nothing moved.

Dan shuddered.

"Goddam Koyukons got 'em," Black Claw muttered. "Tol' you not trust those bastard."

Dan tried to reply, found that his tongue didn't seem to work, his throat wouldn't move in speech.

"Nothing here," he said finally, his voice coming out in a raspy harshness. "Let's go check the village."

"Better be careful. Might still be there."

There were a number of new graves on the little bluff above the river, and among these were the markers for Deriabin and Bernard. Most of the Russian post had been burned, and only one representative of the Russian-American Company remained—Ivan Pavloff, the Creole trader. He had come up from Redoubt St. Michael when word had reached the settlement of the massacre. He had been in Nulato for perhaps a month.

But it was from Salmon Berry that Locke and Black Claw first learned what had happened during February.

"Was Red Bear's warriors did this, Luckydan. Kill almost everybody, kill Gossack chief and Prettycoat Lieutenant. Kill both my sons. . . ."

Black Claw moved forward silently, put his arms around the woman. She leaned wearily against him for a few moments, then straightened.

"Loon-cry . . . ?" Dan asked, his voice shaking.

"I don' think she dead, Luckydan. They hit me over head, must of thought they killed me. I look all over next day, saw lots of bodies, but not Loon-cry, not your little one. They probably take her, pretty young woman, baby. Ever'body like pretty young woman, baby."

"How long ago . . . ?" Dan asked, sweeping his hand vaguely toward the fort, the village.

"Three moons, maybe. Lose track," she said. "Hudson Bay, friend of Prettycoat, he come few days later, bury people from fort. Prettycoat, he still alive then, but he die too. People in my village, they down in kashims, nobody to bury them. Bunch run away, come back afterward. Snow Flower an' me, we can't do nothin', we just women."

Locke bent his head, pressed his fingers against his forehead, unable to comprehend everything Salmon Berry told him.

She said Loon-cry, Naomi, said they're alive, though. . . .

"I sorry, Luckydan," Salmon Berry whispered. "Keep thinkin' I could of done something. . . . Pretty soon we all move somewhere. Live with Ingaliks and Ikogmiuts, maybe. Goddam Red Bear. . . ."

Dan shook his head weakly, and Black Claw drew the widow into his arms once again.

Standing behind her was her widowed daughter-in-law Snow Flower, a young one still in arms, a girl perhaps six months of age. She had been wife to Salmon Berry's younger son, and the pain of loss was still etched deeply into both women's faces.

* * *

The American grimly stowed his furs in one of the remaining sheds, accepted Ivan Pavloff's tally sheet without comment, and made preparations for a desperate venture upriver to find Red Bear's village. Such a course of action would be, as Pavloff insisted, little more than an elaborate means of committing suicide, but Dan was not to be dissuaded.

Locke shook his head.

"Guess you're right, Ivan. Don't make no difference, though. If Loon-cry and my kid are still alive, then I got to go find them, whatever the Gawddamned odds against me. That short-necked bastard knows me—I've run afoul of him before. There's no question—Loon's told him whose woman she is. And that means Red Bear's expecting me. I tell you, I'll wrestle Gawd one-on-one if there's a chance in hell of getting her back. Don't go telling me there's other females. Don't you understand? I've flat got to go up there, no matter what. Without her, it just ain't worth living. . . ."

He loaded his canoe with every bit of cargo it would hold, exhausting a good portion of Pavloff's meager stock: multicolored blankets, pots, pans, steel needles, various colored spools of thread, a dozen knives of differing sorts, vermilion, steel spear points, two full bags of dried beans and wheat flour, blue canvas, a brace of old fusees and a supply of powder and lead, and a naval field glass.

These things, he hoped, might serve as a kind of ransom—a bride price in the mind of the Koyukon chief.

Pavloff cooperated but looked dour.

Black Claw shook his head and repeatedly muttered, "Crazy White devil."

"We found Bulegin's remains—our upriver trader," Pavloff said. "The flesh all charred, and nothin' left of arms and legs but the bones. . . ."

"Salmon Berry says they cooked poor bastard, ate him, had helluva feast, hokay. That's what she hear from gossip friends at Toklat. Upriver Koyukons, they chew on your legs too, Luckydan. Goddam, stay with us. At least I don' eat you."

Locke shrugged.

"Gents," he said, "I'm dead inside right now. Fate gutted me, an' I'm no damned good to myself or anybody else. You know as well as I do that Naomi's up there—Koyukons nor anybody else kills children. The tribes have been stealing little ones from each other since time began, an' that's a fact. Women the same way—there's probably half a dozen bucks wanting Loon-cry for their woman, if Red Bear himself hasn't taken her. Give this scow of mine a shove. Ivan, if I don't make it back, Black Claw gets what's left of my shares."

Pavloff nodded.

"Don' want Goddam shares . . . ," the scar-faced one muttered.

Back on the river once more, moving upstream over the same course that he and Black Claw had so recently navigated in the opposite direction, his canoe low in the water but still gliding along to the rhythmic *slish-slish, slish-slish* of his double-bladed paddle.

Fifty miles to the Koyukon confluence—another fifty, according to reports of questionable authority, to a broad point of land just south of the Kateel mouth—and there he would find Red Bear's village, the primary encampment of the warrior people who controlled the entire northwest interior as far as Schwatka Mountains and beyond.

Even during good times, the Russians stayed south of Koyukon River, where the unfortunate Bulegin had been temporarily stationed at a makeshift trading post for the benefit of Red Bear's people. Long before the massacre, two parties of *promyshlenniki* ventured north of Koyukon mouth, and not so much as a single one of the trappers ever returned. Red Bear's people were generally willing to tolerate Russian presence and to make use of the trading post at Nulato, but Gossacks who ventured beyond that point were now believed to be as good as dead.

Had Dan known what he now knew with regard to the disposition of the northern Koyukons, he reflected, he'd never have brought that H.B.C. brigade down into the eastern portion of their lands—but because he had done that, Hans Larsson was dead.

Red Bear.

The son of a bitch had Loon-cry and little Naomi.

"Well, Mike McLafferty, I was only a greenhorn when I whipped you at your own game—bluffed you, by Gawd, and took in the pot. Couldn't have done it a second time, of course—and you had the tin to wear me down in a long game. You didn't, though. Just grinned and tipped your silly Mexican hat and sauntered off. Gawddamn it, I'll bluff my way into Red Bear's village, too, and one way or another I'm going to come out of there alive, my woman and my kid with me. Make a man desperate enough, and he'll take on half a dozen Koyukon tribes. . . . You just watch, McLafferty, an' this coon'll show you how it's done."

Locke burst out laughing.

"Talking to a figment—boasting to a gambling man who likely don't even remember me and who was maybe setting me up for a bigger game later on, only we never got around to playing it."

Living mists of gnats and mosquitoes drifted in shady places along the Kuikpak's banks, and down beneath the surface, finning along through silt-laden water, were the grayling, the pike, the whitefish, the inconnu. . . .

He could feel their silent, mysterious presence.

Lucky Dan Locke, the Boston, the Gringo.

Crazy Goddam White devil got heap medicine.

Hell yes.

Red Bear, you mud-footed son of a bitch, you may have half the damned North Country shitting its britches, but you ain't tangled with this Yank yet.

Heavy clouds were running in from the south, and as Locke turned away from the main channel into the tributary Koyukon a lancing rain began to fall—striking the surface of the gray-green water like some ubiquitous blast of shotgun pellets.

Rain in his face, rainwater dripping from his beard, rain driven on the wind and penetrating even his heavy leathers. . . .

He fought the weather for an hour or so longer but finally turned his prow shoreward, gliding into the cove of a tributary creek and pulling his craft up onto the shore amidst a tangle of bunchgrass and yellow-centered purple Arctic crocuses.

Dan checked the tarp lashings to assure himself there would be no water damage to the merchandise he carried and then, Hawken in hand, strode off through clusters of white-capped sphagnum and tall-stemmed fireweed toward a heavy grove of elder and aspen. Here he rigged up a storm blanket and, using a small quantity of black powder and his steel and flint, he kindled a fire—even though there were still several hours of daylight remaining.

"It's a good day to die," he chuckled, not at all certain why he was in such high spirits, "it's a good place to die, and a damned good reason to die as well."

He heaped chunks of deadwood on his blaze and took curious delight in watching the smoke plume upward and finally vanish in the continuing rainfall.

Still forty miles, more or less, to Red Bear's village—but it was nonetheless possible that some wandering Koyukon would see his fire.

"Be good to have a bit of company at that," Lucky Dan mused as he pulled out a full flask of what Pavloff advertised as good Kiev vodka—more likely the product of distilled rotten potato juice at Petropavlovsk in Kamchatka, one way of making something out of the remnants of winter's supply.

He tipped the flask to his lips, drank, blinked several times, and coughed. After a moment or two he realized that he could actually breathe once more.

"Damn fine rotgut," he chuckled. "Black Claw would enjoy this brew—no question about 'er. Wish the old bastard was here—just didn't want him getting killed on my account, that's all. I've already done enough damage to him for one lifetime. . . . Why in hell'd I have to end up actually liking that loud-mouthed clown? You murder a man's son, you don't want to turn him into your damned uncle. . . ."

He drank again, snorted, drank some more.

After a time Locke set a caribou steak to sizzling over the flames, smoked his pipe, had a couple more drinks, and then began to eat the meat, even though it was no more than half done.

"Cook meat too much," he reflected, "and you get the scurvy. Eat 'er raw, and you never will. . . ."

He tilted back the flask three more times and cursed happily when the vodka was gone.

Lucky Dan staggered to his fire, piled more wood on, and then pulled his blankets about his shoulders, leaned back against an elder, and passed out.

* * *

Two days later, and grimly sober, Dan Locke brazenly pulled his canoe ashore at the main landing of the Koyukon village. Half a dozen Koyukon warriors and three young boys stood by, grinning and puzzled, as the solitary Whiteman turned to them, indicated by means of hand signs that he wished them to unload his canoe, and then, using his best Nulato dialect, told them the presents were for Chief Red Bear.

One of the boys immediately ran off toward the village on the bluff above, while the remaining Koyukons, arms folded across their chests, stood motionless.

Dan cursed in English and then in French and Russian, pointed to the loaded canoe, and demanded in Nulato dialect that they begin unloading the cargo.

At length a couple of the men gave in and did as they were directed, glancing at their peers and then scowling at Lucky Dan.

So far, so good. If my luck holds, I may even still be alive in five minutes. . . .

The prescribed five minutes passed.

Then Red Bear appeared. If anything, Dan noted, the old warrior looked even more fierce than the last time he'd seen the son of a bitch.

Locke stared directly into Red Bear's eyes.

"Your men took my woman captive—she was at Nulato last winter when you and your warriors killed the Russians and those who worked for them. Loon-cry, the Kutchin. And my daughter, Naomi. I have come to buy them back, Red Bear."

"I remember you," the chief said. "You bury your friend. Damned stupid. Still that way."

"I bring these things as a bride price, even though Loon-cry is my own wife. Guns, blankets, spear points, knives, things for the women. . . ."

"You offer me only what I could take anyway, Boston. You an' your men steal furs from Koyukon lands. Probably I going to kill you now."

The eyes on that bastard—like Gawddamn brown holes in the snow—only hard, mud-colored obsidian. He's not merely in a position to win the card game, he owns the cards. What in hell have I got to put on the table? Should have listened to Black Claw and Ivan the Terrible. . . .

"I have been told the Koyukons are skilled wrestlers, but I do not believe it. I challenge you, Red Bear. I bring you gifts, and yet you threaten to steal them from me. You may kill me because you have your warriors to help you, but you could not do it alone. Perhaps when you were younger, but now? Well, I would have defeated you even then, I suppose. . . ."

"Loyalty to dead friend is stupid, Boston. Come here to try take woman back, even more stupid. Ugly white face with hair on it. Maybe I have you burned."

"I have come for my woman and my child, Red Bear."

Staring directly at the powerful Koyukon and without hesitating, Lucky Dan drew his Colt Walker pistol and directed it at Red Bear's chest.

"Same trick as last time, eh, Luckydan? Loon-cry say you come, but I didn't think you that stupid. Got bear turds for brains, that's what I think. Raven Man, he takes care of people like you, I guess. Red Bear accepts your gifts, but can't give you woman. She belongs to Blue Weasel now. You want to wrestle somebody, that right? You wrestle the Weasel then. Lose, I let him slit your throat while woman watches. Win, you take Loon-cry and little girl and go downriver. Ever come back again, we have you for feast—find out if Yengee taste good as Gossack."

Lucky Dan nodded his assent, thrust his pistol back into his belt, and followed Red Bear toward the Koyukon village.

9

Blue Weasel

The warriors were summoned, and many of the women and children crowded around as well. Red Bear spoke to his people, explaining to them what was about to transpire.

"Where is Blue Weasel? I order him to come—bring Loon-cry and little girl with him. He must wrestle this Beard-face, otherwise give woman and child to him. The Boston is brave man, not smart man. He comes here because Loon-cry is his wife—he wishes her returned. Brings me presents. Bull's Piz-zle and Honker, they carrying things up here. Dan Locke, he gives 'em to me. I give 'em to Blue Weasel if he defeats the Boston an' cuts his throat."

Lucky Dan stripped off his leathers and even went so far as to flex his muscles for the benefit of the onlookers—presuming, reasonably enough, that some benefit might accrue in attempting to engage the general acceptance if not the sym-pathies of the Koyukon people.

Red Bear, suddenly looking not fierce at all, began to grin and then to laugh.

"Covered with fur, like skinny shedding black toklat!" Honker said, laying down the bundle he'd just hauled up from the landing.

At this point a huge individual pushed through the throng, dragging Loon-cry along with him. He too was naked to the waist, but his torso was marked with jagged stripes of black and white paint.

"Danl-ock! I knew you come, just like before. This man, Blue Weasel, he want me for wife, but I don' do it. . . ."

The sight of her, the sound of her voice. . . . For an instant Lucky Dan was not even slightly interested in the ungainly and grotesque Koyukon. He turned instead toward Loon-cry, began to walk toward her.

"Loon-love, Gawddamn it gal, I had to come. . . ."

"Watch out, Danl-ock!"

Then a blood-curdling scream of rage, and Blue Weasel's weight was upon him, driving him forward as he sought to regain his balance.

One arm around my throat, blind-sided me, the cheating son of a bitch. . . .

Suddenly filled with a proper Yankee sense of moral out-rage, Dan dropped to both knees and tumbled forward, using the Koyukon's weight and momentum against him, and landing with the man beneath him.

Blue Weasel struggled for breath, released his hold around Dan's neck.

Locke was up instantly, striking the same sort of banty rooster pose that he and his schoolmates had used years earlier in Missouri. He grinned, paraded back and forth, even bowed to the throng that formed a circle about him.

Loon-cry, staring straight at me. Trying to give this child strength. Can't let her down now—got to keep hold of myself. Blind lucky on that move, and could of got myself killed.

Blue Weasel rose to one knee, still struggling to regain the breath that had been knocked out of him.

Texas rules. . . .

Dan slammed a resounding kick into Blue Weasel's side, sending him to hands and knees once again, and then delivered a forehand smash to the side of the head.

Again the Koyukon attempted to rise, and again Locke took advantage of the situation. What, after all, were rules of fair play? No one, certainly, had mentioned any—nor did the onlookers seem particularly outraged by what he'd done thus far. With such a thought in mind, hardly conscious in any case, Locke fell upon his man, grabbing him by the long hair and repeatedly driving his face into the ground.

With Blue Weasel now groggy, Dan used the hair to pull him halfway to his feet, brought up one knee, and sent the Koyukon sprawling.

Red Bear, who had been studying Dan's tactics quite carefully, now tossed a long-bladed knife onto the ground at Locke's feet.

What in hell?

Then Dan realized the significance of the action. The chief was granting permission for him to take the beaten warrior's life.

He gestured to the chief, shook his head, and kicked the knife to one side.

"Boston Yengee wins," Red Bear said loudly enough so that all might hear. "Loon-cry the Kutchin, you must fetch your child and go with this man—you must do that unless you wish to stay with me. Blue Weasel shows he unworthy of you."

But as Loon-cry started across the opening where the two men had wrestled only a few moments earlier, apparently intent upon embracing her husband, Blue Weasel was on his feet. In his hand was the knife that Lucky Dan had kicked away.

In the next long, agonizing, and almost timeless moment, the knife arced down, plunging into Loon-cry's flesh just to one side of the vee of her throat. She fell without a sound, her face striking the earth, and immediately a pool of blood began to form.

Blue Weasel, screaming, stumbled toward Lucky Dan.

For a moment Locke stood as one transfixed—certain what he had seen could not have happened, certain it was all a horrible nightmare in which one lived out his worst and most terrible fears.

No!

Unarmed though he was, he threw himself forward, driving his head into Blue Weasel's midsection just as the knife descended, the point gouging into his lower back and jamming against his hip girdle.

Pain, sensation, a small voice in the back of his mind said, would come within a few seconds. Pain, but he was not seriously wounded. Hardly aware of his opponent's weight, Locke spun the man, hurled him to the earth. Then Dan dived for his leathers and the Colt Walker pistol.

When Blue Weasel regained his feet, Lucky Dan was standing before him, weapon raised.

The explosion was a whiplash of sound, gunsmoke rising in the air, and the .44 slug hit the big Koyukon directly in the center of his chest. For a moment Blue Weasel stood there, grinning confusedly—but then the strength went out of him, and he sagged back to the ground.

Dan turned, pointing his weapon now at one, now at another of the men in the tightening circle.

"Do not kill anyone else, Boston Dan," Red Bear commanded, gesturing with open hands. "You do no more than honor demands. Now it is over. This terrible thing—didn't mean for it to happen. Loon-cry is dead. I cannot give her to you because she is gone."

"Dead?"

"She goes with Raven Man now. I send Honker to get your little one, Luckydan. I will not keep things you bring as presents because I cannot pay you for them. You must take your child and leave my village—leave in safety. Brave man,

stupid man. Why not kill Blue Weasel? I gave him to you. . . .
Then none of this happen."

Dead? Loon-cry dead?

"Where is she? I must see her . . . her body. . . ."

"The Kutchin woman is already with Raven Man. Bull's
Pizzle and New Spear, they carry things back to canoe. Honker
brings little girl. You go in peace, Luckydan. Never come back
to this place. If you do, I have you burned to death. Hear my
words, Whiteman. Go now."

Locke, given no opportunity to object—to assert that he
would take Loon-cry's remains with him, would give her a
proper burial, lowered his pistol and thrust it back into his
belt. Strong hands pushed at his back, his shoulders.

His own blood, spattered down one leg of his leather
trousers, and now a terrific, grinding ache near the small of
his back. Unceremoniously he was guided and cudgeled back
down the slope to his canoe at river's edge.

The trade goods were lashed into place, and Locke was
assisted into his craft.

His Hawken rifle—it was still there. He leaned forward
to reach for the gun, felt the hot sensation of pain from his
back. And then a hand grasped his forearm.

"Leave gun alone, White devil!"

Dan stared into the face of the Koyukon called Bull's
Pizzle.

"You brave somabitch but no brain in head," the Indian
said, "just like Red Bear says. Don' come back here no more.
We don' want kill you, Luckydan. Loon-cry, she tell my wife
about you—how you kidnap her, kill husband, marry her. You
good man. Go away now."

Within a short while the warrior called Honker appeared.
Standing beside him was a short, round-faced woman whose
aspect and general demeanor suggested that she fully expected
all manner of horrors to descend upon her—she was clearly
terror-stricken. Wordlessly she continued to shake her head
as she clutched at a child—and the child wore a silver crucifix
about her throat. Little Naomi, Naomi Walks-Between-Worlds,
Dan realized in the next instant.

A moment thereafter Red Bear himself appeared.

"This woman named Dancing Rabbit," the chief said. "Blue
Weasel's wife. You kill him—now she's yours. Take her and
go, Boston."

Dan studied the face of the stricken woman, the grim expression of the men who stood behind her.

"Give me my daughter as you promised, Red Bear. I do not want the dead man's wife. Bring me instead the body of the woman I love . . . I wish to . . . bury her in the proper way. . . ."

"Dead one stay here. Don't want Dancing Rabbit? Take the little one, then, and go away."

Naomi, bound to a carrying board by means of otterskin straps, screamed wretchedly as she was passed into Dan's arms—continued to scream, her enraged cries echoing over the broad Koyukon River waters as Red Bear's warriors, wading out a short way, pushed the canoe ahead of them and gave the craft a final brisk shove.

There was nothing else to do, and Locke dipped his paddle, then again, again. . . .

Numbness. Unreality. A lost man and a screaming child drifting on the darkening currents of an Arctic river. Nothing that made sense. Horror swirling in the mists that rose around them as they moved toward midstream current and made their way southward toward . . . what? No family, no solace, no help—toward a world punctuated merely by the mournful cries of owls and a distant sound of crickets.

Through mists alternating with thin starlight the canoe moved. At length little Naomi cried herself to sleep, and Dan ceased to paddle, stowed his blade aboard, and tucked another blanket in about the child.

Disturbed by his movements, Naomi awoke once more and once more began to cry.

"Loon, Gawddamn it, wherever you are, tell me what to do. I done my best, Loon, I thought I was doing right—and Gawddamn it, my own stupidity got you killed. I'm guilty, guilty, Gawd forgive this child. Help me now, Loon. I can feel you close around me—I know you want to. You're the mother —I can feel you trying to tell this dumbass Yank what to do. Damn it, how can I feed her? She's all I got left, Loon-cry, all I got left of you. . . ."

Sugar.

He fumbled through his possibles sack, withdrew the small watertight canister. He placed four or five lumps into a clean kerchief, tied them into place, and dampened the whole thing.

He leaned forward, touched a finger to his daughter's lips, and felt the little one relax slightly in anticipation.

Yes, she's hoping for Loon's breast. . . . My Gawd, this is killing me. Got to hang on—can't go crazy yet, not with you depending on me, Naomi child. I've got to hang on.

He placed the wrapped sugar lumps to the child's mouth. Her hands struggled upward from under the blankets, and she grasped the kerchief, began to suck at it.

"Did I do right, Loon-love? Gawddamn it, gawddamn it, I ain't up to this—but I gotta be, don't I? Help me, Loon. How could I have left you back there—too shocked to think right? Dead. How do I even know that? No matter what Red Bear said to me, how in hell did I really know? Aw, shit, I'm out of my mind, clutching at straws in the wind. Got to hold on here."

Mists rose up ahead of him on the dark river, dimly visible, dark forms of shifting dimension—and for one brief moment she was there. Loon-cry, her face hovering above him.

The sobs that he had somehow held back now broke through the shell of grim resolve that had been shielding his sanity, his control, his capacity to act rationally. They came in gasps of pain—of torment, of loss, of guilt, of all these things together. He screamed into the fog as though under torture. . . . Knife blades gouged into his guts, the blades twisting, and dull, humbling, deadening fire ran through him.

Grown man and infant child drifting down a dark river, and both of them wailing in rage and despair.

A soft, warm rain began to fall the following day about noon, but Dan continued down the twisting Koyukon. Naomi, shielded by a flap of canvas pulled tight from the bundled trade goods and laced into place, slept soundly for several hours—so soundly, in fact, that Dan found himself on more than one occasion leaning forward to assure himself that the little girl was still breathing. When she finally came fully awake and began to scream her lungs out, Dan glanced up into the rain and muttered a distinct *thank you.*

The rain continued to fall, gaining in intensity late in the afternoon as he reached the big, thickly wooded island about which the Koyukon forked before merging with the Lot of Water.

Realizing that Naomi simply had to have something other than sugar lumps to suck on and was without question in need of having the packing in her pants changed, Dan landed his canoe and pulled the craft up onto a pebbled beach where numerous heaps of driftwood had been driven by the floods of a month earlier.

At the upper end of the beach was a large downed spruce, its roots sticking into the air like so many arthritic fingers. Dan strung his storm blanket from these and quickly got a fire blazing while young Naomi sucked disconsolately on yet another wrapped sugar lump.

The small canister, Dan noted, was nearly empty.

What to feed the little devil?

Locke cut shavings of jerky into his coffee pot, dipped water from an ooze at the shingle's marge, and set the brew in against the flames. Nearby were some wild onions, and he pulled these—added them to the broth.

Am I doing this right, Loon-cry? Gawdamn it, gal, I know you didn't desert me . . . I know that. Jesus Christ, it was my fault, what happened. If I hadn't shown that son of a bitch common mercy, you'd be alive an' with me. Loon. . . .

The child's face was red and appeared swollen, her eyes shut tight as she screamed with hunger and discomfort.

He poured some juice out into a cup, blew on it, swirled it about, and finally judged it cool enough. Then, clumsily, he removed her from her carrying board and held her in his arms, pressing her small head forward and holding the cup to her lips—he felt even more helpless than before when she redoubled her screams and thrashed about.

"You drink, damn it!" he shouted, giving vent to his own frustration.

Inexplicably, at the sound of the loud male voice, the infant quieted instantly and stared up at the gaunt, bearded face. The lips curled as if in preparation for further crying, but then the child sucked with clumsy eagerness at the thin soup, dribbled most of it down her face, but swallowed some.

She took a few more sips, relaxed, lapsed into sleep for a minute or two, and then accepted more nourishment.

When she was finished, Dan cleaned her and changed her, feeling strangely hesitant as he ministered to the small woman-child, hesitant and terribly clumsy as well. But he persevered, and finally the child, tense lines in the round face vanished, slept peacefully. Dan wrapped her in one of his old shirts and scooped out a small hollow for her in the gravelly sand perhaps two feet from the fire.

His task completed, he chewed on jerky and drank from his final small container of Pavloff's vodka. After several drinks and yet another fit of sobbing, Dan rose and walked back to his canoe. He stared out into the rainy air and forming mists and called out to the woman he loved, the woman he'd lost.

No more than the sound of soft rain, of turbid and swirling current, of the rapid clatter of mallard wings somewhere downstream, beyond where the river channel bent.

He withdrew his Colt Walker, stared at the weapon, checked the cylinder. Without hesitation he raised the pistol to his temple, closed his eyes, and drew back the hammer.

But at this instant he heard Naomi beginning to cry once more. Quickly he thrust the revolver back under his belt, ashamed of himself and the desperate act of weakness he'd been about to perform. Momentarily, he was shocked to realize, he'd forgotten totally about his child.

"I'm coming!" he called out and began to jog back to where the storm blanket was fastened to the upthrust roots of a fallen spruce.

He was back in Red Bear's village, and at its center a huge fire was burning. A Russian functionary, nothing left of his face but a broad grin, raised a shot glass filled with vodka, drank it off, and then marched briskly into the fire. He climbed onto a huge spit that had been placed at the fire's center and wrapped himself about it, clinging there with hands and feet. A moment later he turned into a pig with an apple stuck in its mouth, and savory odors of roasting flesh drifted through the afternoon air.

The Koyukon people danced in unison, danced to the rhythm of a drum, its hollow sounds punctuated every so often by the screamings of birds and the howls of wolves.

The people, Dan realized, were extremely happy. They flung their arms about one another's shoulders and skipped sideways, their feet flashing through intricate designs.

Loon-cry was there, and a raven perched upon the top of her head. She smiled and looked directly into his eyes, but the smile betrayed some deep inner sadness.

He attempted to call to her, but no words formed. When he approached her, she turned away, walking off toward the dark spruce forest. The black bird was fanning its wings, and yet it did not lift off into the air.

He began to run after her, but then his feet grew heavy —heavy, as though he were fighting his way through snow-drifts.

He was alone. The Koyukons had all vanished. The fire was gone. And at the far side of the village, where Loon-cry had disappeared, a grizzly bear stood on its hind legs, and the creature was waving its arms back and forth.

A child was crying.

Naomi.

Dan rose, put the remainder of the wood he'd gathered onto the dwindling fire, and pushed the pot of broth in close to the coals.

He turned then, lifted the child, held her to his chest, and stroked her hair.

"Naomi," he whispered. "Gawddamn it, girl, we've got problems, both of us. But we got each other, at least. We got that. I don't know much of anything about raising a kid, but I'll give 'er a try. Somehow or another, we got to stick together. Your momma, well, she lives as long as we remember her . . . but you're so young, not even a year yet. I'm your daddy, but you don't remember me . . . I been gone, I was gone when the Koyukons come into Nulato. And now Loon-cry's gone, but she ain't going to come back. She didn't choose that, you understand. No, it's that she . . . damn it, she got taken away . . . I don't rightly know where. You're hungry, aren't you? And here I am blabbering like I had good sense or you could understand me even if I did. Let's try you on some more of this broth. Another day, with luck, and we'll be back to Nulato. Salmon Berry's daughter-in-law, what's her name? Snow Flower, yes, and she's got a little one—probably enough milk to get you on for a time. And she'll know how to do the things that I don't, Naomi. It's going to be all right. Honest to Gawd. . . ."

Fifty miles downriver to Nulato.

Dan walked up from the landing, Naomi in his arms, and proceeded directly to Salmon Berry's lodge. Black Claw was there, squinting with his one good eye.

"Loon-cry?" he asked—and Dan knew the old Kutchin already understood what the answer would be.

"Gone. So close—so close to getting her back. One of the sons of bitches, I wrestled him and won, but then. . . ."

Salmon Berry and Snow Flower emerged from the kashim.

"My daughter needs to be fed," Dan whispered hoarsely. "Flower . . . could you?"

The young widow glanced at her mother-in-law and at Black Claw, then smiled, nodded.

"I take her," she said. "Salmon Berry and I, we do everything needs to be done. Don't you worry, Luckydan. Loon-cry, she help me when my baby comes. Now I help her, help however I can."

Dan nodded his thanks, handed his infant daughter to the woman.

"Dead?" Salmon Berry asked. "How . . . ?"

"Murdered," Dan replied. "I'll explain the whole thing. I've fed Naomi as best I could on the way down the river, but—hell, I don't know what I'm doing. I need to sleep for about two weeks, and then. . . ."

"What you goin' do?" Black Claw asked.

"Old friend," Locke replied, "to tell the truth, I haven't got the slightest damned idea in the world. Maybe . . . later . . . I'll be able to get my wits together."

Of those who had survived the winter attack by Red Bear and his warriors, some had actually gone upriver to join the Koyukons, while others had drifted away off into the taiga, choosing to live anywhere so long as it was at some distance from the village where such death and destruction had visited.

Ivan Pavloff and half a dozen Creole employees of Russian-American Company would remain for another month or two to complete company business, trading for yet a few more furs that might be brought in, and then they would leave as well, and they too would journey by raft and canoe down the Kuikpak to the mission post at Ikogmut, leaving Nulato itself to prowling wolves and the storms of winter.

Lucky Dan hired the widowed Snow Flower to care for Naomi and to breast-feed her—something that would continue, in accord with native cultural habit, at least until the child's second birthday. When summer came, and the child's health was restored, Locke announced his intention of parting company with Black Claw and Salmon Berry, who had elected to remain, for a short time at least, in the by now nearly deserted village of Nulato.

"You don't go, Luckydan," Black Claw protested. "All of us, we go back up Lot of Water to Fort Youcan. You work for Murray and Alexander. I trap with you, maybe. We do good, hokay, just like last time. Naomi, she needs father. I'm like grandfather, but maybe I get old an' die pretty soon—then Naomi, she's orphan, like one who is gone. Snow Flower—she's good mother, you see that. You marry Snow Flower, an' then both little ones have mother an' father."

"I'm taking Naomi with me, old friend. Snow Flower too, but not to marry her. She's agreed to go down to Ikogmut. The Cossacks have a church there, and I'll provide quarters and leave sufficient money with the priest to take care of both of them until next summer. I've got to go away for a time— I don't know where. Black Claw, I still feel Loon-cry's death hovering about me. Things have all gone empty for me—got to be somewhere else until my wits come back to me. I love the North Country, and maybe even the violence—maybe even that. But this time that damned Raven Man's stuck his beak right into my heart. My *yeg*, it's been wounded. Needs time to heal. As things are, I can't even sleep—keep dreaming, waking up. It's killing me, and I've got to get away for a time."

"You know about this?" Black Claw demanded of Salmon Berry.

The Nulato woman nodded.

"Snow Flower, she tell me. Ask me what I think. Guess Dan's right, guess so. When alder leaves go yellow, I think we come down to Ikogmut too—only Black Claw, he want to go back to his people, way up where river comes from. Maybe I go with him, don' know. . . ."

Black Claw rose, fumbled about for his stone pipe, filled the bowl with tobacco, lit it with a glowing twig end.

"Ain't good, hokay," he said after he'd puffed two or three times. "Luckydan, you take Snow Flower with you, then you got to be like her husband anyhow. Better you marry her, jus' like I'm goin' to marry Salmon Berry, here. Then we all be family. You an' me, we trap together. I even promise not to kill you like I always said I was goin' to."

Dan rose, hugged the old warrior.

"Stop actin' like man-woman," Black Claw grumbled. "I don' want to go to bed with no crazy Goddam White devil Boston Yengee."

Locke persisted in his design, however, and the following day he was once again back on the river, moving away southward toward the Russian settlements at Kaltag and Ikogmut. The young widow Snow Flower was with him—and her child and little Naomi as well.

A gentle east wind was blowing, fretting the river's broad surface with ripples, and black-headed Canadian geese were swarming in the shallows and knifing along through the air in flocks of thirty or more, the big birds apparently enjoying the warmth of northern summer.

Dan glanced at his young daughter—noted that the chubby little hands were busily if futilely engaged in attempting to unfasten the otterskin bindings that held her to her backboard.

"Since she learned how to walk," Dan grinned, "she just doesn't have much patience with being held down."

Snow Flower smiled, nodded. She unfastened her leather blouse and drew up her own daughter and placed the child's mouth at her breast.

Naomi turned as well as she could to see what the other little one was doing, struggled momentarily, and then looked back pleadingly at her father.

"Danl-ock," the child said, the sound strung out so as to be more or less indecipherable.

For a long moment Locke stared at her.

"You hear that?" he demanded.

"Your name," Snow Flower nodded. "Naomi been tryin' to say it several days now."

10

Redoubt St. Michael

"*Dah, ehtah vahzhnah*, yes, it's important, Daniel, Father Netzvetov and I will see to it that little Naomi receives the best of care," Father Georgi assured Lucky Dan. "And Snow Flower is welcome, as well, if she wishes to stay on with us. I sense a hunger in her for spiritual values, something rare among God's children of this Northland. I hope, in fact, that someday she will choose the way of the cross, perhaps even serve as a witness to others of her people. And your daughter, as well, will be taught to love Our Lord, to the extent of her understanding, of course. I'm sure that is what you would wish? I cannot tell you how it raised my spirits to see the beautiful crucifix she wears. It reminded me of God's love for all his little ones, even here in this wilderness. Well, I go on, but I'm sure you want to be on your way. Please be assured that we will do our best for your daughter. . . ."

Dan Locke glanced up the hill to the still not-quite-finished church behind the village, the structure topped by a blue onion dome and three double crosses, officially consecrated to the Holy Life-Giving Cross just the previous December and symbolizing the long struggle of Netzvetov's ministry—that strange, taciturn Creole scholar who had actually translated portions of the Gospel into his native Aleut tongue.

Netzvetov was not a man one easily got to know, Locke reflected, but Father Georgi was a different breed of dog. As a foreigner, he was nonetheless far more tolerant of those he found within his care. As a result of discussions Dan had with the priest at one time or another since arriving at Ikogmut, Locke had come to understand that Georgi's devout nature was far more in tune with the natural rhythms of the wildness

111

around him than it was with the strict dictates of the church. Georgi gloried in such things as the breakup of Kuikpak ice in the spring, in the luxuriance of spring flowers, in the trumpetings of elk, and in the bounding, almost fluid movements of caribou on the run.

Father Georgi, in short, was Locke's kind of man of the cloth, even if he was a damned Russki.

But after all, Lucky Dan had long since concluded, the good or the evil of individual men had little or nothing to do with either their race or their presumed beliefs.

Now, with Loon-cry dead and with his entire previous life little more than a blur, a blur made coherent only by the fact of his daughter Naomi's existence, Dan Locke found that he could take solace in the obvious concern etched upon the face of this bearded Russian priest—himself alone and a stranger far from the land of his birth.

Now, indeed, Dan found that he missed even that old reprobate, Black Claw—the man's laughter and continual hints that he yet intended to kill Locke in order to honor the memory of Raven's Egg. . . . *Memories, merely blurred memories, the unlikely outworkings of fate, and all of it played before the amused audience of Raven Man, that half-crazed spirit of life and of death as well.* . . .

"*Spahsoobah*, I thank you," Lucky Dan said, shaking hands with the priest. "I don't think you believe me when I say it, but by golly I'll say it again anyway. I will be back. Just got to get things straightened around first, that's all. Then I'm taking my daughter with me—to the United States, maybe to California, maybe far to the east of there, where the Missouri River comes looping down out of the prairies. I want to go home—does that sound foolish for a grown man to be saying it?"

"*Nyet*, my son, your words are not foolish at all. I too, at times, yearn to be back home in Mother Russia. I'm obliged to obey the dictates of the Church, however, and thus I remain here. So I tell myself. But at other times *home* seems to me to be precisely Ikogmut village, here beside the great river—the sheer innocence and wildness of the place, the smoldering souls of these people who have been given into my care. . . . We do, finally, what we must. I will look forward to seeing you again, then, at the time when the day and the night are equal. Until then, Daniel Locke the American, go in the blessing of the Holy Trinity. Let that protect you in your continuing *esnaih*."

Yes.

Back on the river, riding the great river of the North Country, its silt-laden current carrying him toward the cold Bering Sea.

He was a man adrift, rootless, a wanderer. Where the hell he was bound for or why he had no idea—just a need for time sufficient to sort out his thoughts and to get over, if that were possible, the haunting brown eyes and delicately formed facial features of a young Kutchin woman who called him Danl-ock for no reason that he had ever been able to discern, inasmuch as her English had been generally quite good. The way she said it—as though she were tasting the sounds, turning first and last names into one name, the first syllable gliding into the second.

Dead. Either buried in permafrost so that her remains would no doubt keep virtually forever, or else consumed in fire so that her flesh and, more important, the very being of her had swirled up into the air and was blown on the winds, a bit here, a bit there, until at last Loon-cry would disperse completely and would therefore be everywhere, even in the air he breathed. But, no, not Loon-cry herself. In the beliefs of her people, she would long since have crawled through Raven Man's tunnel and emerged beside the Spirit-Lot-of-Water, and Raven Man would have kept her in his lodge for a time, making love to her until she'd ceased to think of the world she'd left behind, and then those ghostly boatmen would have come across the river for her and have taken her into the land of the dead. Perhaps it was so. Or Father Georgi's God and all his ministering angels—surely the utterly innocent were allowed to enter directly into heaven, if indeed that heaven existed for so pure a child of wild nature as Loon-cry, she who'd never in her life wished to harm anyone or anything and whose very nature was love. . . .

And what of Lucky Dan Locke?

Would the two of them, in some absolutely impossible way, actually meet again—somewhere—somehow? And if that happened, would they recognize one another, be drawn together once again by the very strength of what they had known between them?

Or was it only mating, after all, nothing more than that? The humping of caribou, of chittering squirrels, of howling coyotes and wolves mauling one another and getting stuck together for their trouble? Just something that creatures of flesh and blood were obliged to do in order to ensure that more of their own kind were able to walk or climb or swim or fly about during the years that would come afterward?

Naomi Locke, a halfbreed child now in the care of Russian priests and an Ikogmiut woman named Jenny Winter Seal— and was she better off remaining where she was or with him, Daniel Locke, in his perpetual nomadic wanderings, his *es-naih*, possibly to California, possibly on south to Mexico and a climate as different as could be from this Far North he'd grown to love so dearly?

Because now he had to leave. He knew it. He felt it deep in his guts. Something was gone out of it—all the beauty, all the extravagant intemperateness of this land of Alaska and the Youcan—the spirit of the place—had vanished with the descending arc of a knife and the spilled blood of a woman named Loon-cry.

A new start, then, in some place far away and as different as possible—for maybe then his painful dreams would at last fade, the pain in the pit of his stomach, like a knotted fist pushing in against his heart and liver, perhaps that would also diminish and eventually go away.

Even the thought of release from pain filled him with guilt, disloyalty.

But there was nothing he could have done that he hadn't at least attempted to do—and he had come so close to succeeding. Red Bear's word—had promised safe passage away from the Koyukon village, his wife and his child with him.

Instead he'd stumbled away brokenly, like a drunken man, yes, and clinging to his infant daughter, the child red-faced and screaming in unnamed and inchoate fear.

"San Francisco, Gawddamn it, and I'll try my luck in the goldfields—gold all over the damned place, and fortunes for the fortunate. . . ."

A big black raven swooped past, low to the river, looking him over.

"Gawddamn you!" Locke shouted. "You merciless son of a bitch! But you ain't beat me yet—this is Lucky Dan talking. I whipped Mike McLafferty at cards, and I'll find a way of whipping you, too, you feathered monster! Satan's crow!"

McLafferty? Some human playmate of yours, Danl-ock? You don't even understand what's happened to you—and it isn't over yet. You are not the child of good fortune—only the dead are fortunate. Your time will come. Listen to what the river says, stupid Whiteman. Loon-cry is calling for you to come back. She wishes to know what you've done with her child. . . .

What the Kuikpak was saying. . . .

Broad, silt-laden waters coursing along between low hills and spruce forests and marshes and muskeg stretching away to far horizons, the taiga becoming more sparse, the low hills bare on their rounded tops and laced with heather as the current moved northwestward now to its fanlike delta athwart the cold ocean, empty tundra landscape and bankside spruce and poplar leaning outward like the "sweepers" back on the Missouri and the Mississippi, roots washed clean by the movement of water, a kind of continual hushing sound of heavy current cutting at the earth which contained it. Geese and loons and mudhens on the water, groups of puffins here and there, a family of black bears splashing about and having a great time, a hundred or more bald eagles perched among the branches of cottonwoods or sturdy young willows a few yards back from shore, a pair of Arctic foxes, their erect ears like four exclamation points at the end of morning.

Loon-cry-loon-cry-loon-cry-cry-cry. . . .

"Whatever the river's got to say," Dan growled, "this Yank ain't of a mind to listen. Salt water ahead, by Gawd, and I'm off the man-killin' son of a bitch!"

Eastward now from the mouth of the Apoon Branch and across fifty miles of open sea, the land fifteen miles to starboard. The heavy Youcan canoe was up to the task, barely, yet at times all of Locke's strength and skill at maneuvering his craft were called into play. Nonetheless, he drove forward tirelessly, and after eight hours or so he rounded a cape and continued southward, his canoe sliding through steel-gray waves. Lucky Dan made his way toward the Russian post of Redoubt St. Michael, where, with no more than a bit of good fortune and a few of the British pound notes in his possibles sack, he'd eventually be able to buy passage southward to Nova Archangelisk—and then take berth on an American vessel and thence south to Seattle or San Francisco. And when that happened, certainly, this whole long nightmare would be over.

No, he wouldn't be returning to Ikogmut in the fall. The long trek downriver and across Norton Sound had served to clear his thoughts. Perhaps he wouldn't be returning for a year or more, perhaps not at all. He'd send money, though. One way or another, he'd see to it that his child was taken care of. Father Georgi was a man of honor—he could be trusted to do right by the little girl.

"Naomi, damn it," he muttered as he moved in endlessly repeated rhythm dictated by the twin-bladed paddle in his clenched hands, "you belong in this land, you belong in a world where the Youcan flows. . . ."

The promontory upon which Redoubt St. Michael stood was dead ahead—not more than five or six miles off.

A pair of white gulls had been following him for the past hour, either simply curious or hoping against hope that he still might toss out something upon the gray swells.

"If you're after my soul, friends, you're too late. Done lost it back there somewhere. Before you get any more of me, my fine feathered white vultures, I fully intend to get gloriously drunk on Russian vodka. Fermented potatoes, they say. Well, we'll see."

St. Mike.

Half a dozen peeled log structures huddling within a vertical log palisade, the whole affair perched athwart gray Arctic waters.

Aside from one or two small fishing craft, the embarcadero was empty. Dan pulled his craft up onto the shingle, dragging it along by the tie rope until it rested above the high tide marks. Then he brushed himself off, flexed his nearly numb hands, and strode off toward the post.

The palisade gates were open, and he walked inside the grounds, past a group of thickset Russian-Aleut Creole *promyshlenniki* workers engaged in constructing an addition to one of the large storage sheds. They paid him no particular attention, and he continued toward the largest of the buildings, in front of which a somewhat ragged Russian flag was flying.

Locke asked for and was given a brief audience with Colonel Pieter Dobshansky, post commandant and, so he'd learned from Fathers Georgi and Netzvetov, the recently appointed chief agent for North American operations, second in actual power only to the Russian governor himself.

"*Vighdyeetyeh! Dvyehr'ahtkritah. . . .*"

Lucky Dan entered the office, as bidden, and stood before a large map on the wall as he awaited Dobshansky's appearance. The chart showed detail of the shoreline to the north and west of St. Mike—information that H.B.C. maps did not have. Beyond Norton Sound a great griffin-headed peninsula projected out toward the tip of Siberia, while immediately to the north of St. Michael, distant perhaps fifty and a hundred miles, respectively, were the Eskimo villages of Unalakleet and Skaktoolik. At neither place was a Russian trading post indicated. If the map was correct, then, Kaltag and Nulato were no more than a hundred miles or so inland from Unalakleet—whereas his own journey by water from Nulato to St. Mike had been several times that distance. And a dotted line indicated an overland trade route that branched beyond a point marked Debouch Mountain. . . .

Colonel Dobshansky, stepping briskly, entered the office, scarcely taking note of Locke's presence, and seated himself behind a desk. Dan nodded uneasily, recalling the welcome the Russkies had given him at Nulato, and presented both his letter of character reference and notes of credit as well, his allowance for several packs of furs sold to the company trader at Ikogmut village.

"*Mahyah fahmeeleeyah*," the American said in halting Russian, "my name is Daniel Locke."

Dobshansky read the documents, squinted summarily at the big, bearded American standing before him, put his signature to the company scrip, and replied in English.

"Yengee," the colonel smiled formally and without genuine interest, "what in God's name are you doing here? Jumped ship and been trapping along the Kuikpak, eh? Netzvetov says you were working above Nulato when our Koyukon savages murdered Deriabin, Bernard, and Bulegin—they had that poor bastard for dinner, according to our reports. I gather you were not among those present at the feast . . .*dah?*"

"Red Bear and his tribesmen are not among my friends," Lucky Dan replied. "One of them murdered my wife."

"Indian woman, I take it?"

Locke nodded.

"Well, there are as many of those as a man wants. Sorry to hear about your loss, though . . . Mr. Locke, is it? I see here that Netzvetov has assumed care of your infant child. Well, well. Are you seeking company authorization, then, or what?"

Locke had already decided that he disliked this man rather intensely—though first impressions, he knew well enough, often did not hold up.

"Nope," he replied. "Just permission to remain here at Redoubt St. Michael until a trading ship comes in. Figuring to book passage to Nova Archangelisk and then south to California."

Dobshansky nodded, his thoughts already turning to other matters.

"*Dah, pryeekrahsnah*, fine. . . ."

Lucky Dan left the commandant's office and proceeded to the small tavern where half a dozen uniformed Russians, a few trappers, and four Indians were drinking and talking within the smoky room lighted by several whale oil lamps.

He ordered a flask of vodka and a glass. He drank off two shots of the clear liquid fire, squinted his eyes, breathed deeply, and then took note of the fact that the Indians were in the process of crowding around him.

"Lucky Dan Locke," one of them growled. "You lucky hokay—lucky we don't slit your throat right now."

At that point he recognized one of the men, then all of them.

Good Christ All-mighty, Red Bear's warriors. . . .

Honker, New Spear, Raccoon Mask, and Bull's Pizzle were a trading band. They'd crossed the Koyukon Trail overland from Red Bear's village, no more than a hundred and fifty miles, they insisted, as the Whitemen reckoned distance. To make the same journey by canoe, as Dan had done, required a venture four or five times that long. Now, having concluded their bartering, they were in process of enjoying the prerogatives of their adventure—to wit, plenty to drink followed directly by a visit to the makeshift whorehouse at the post's perimeter, where two Creole women and four Malemiut Eskimo women made a scant living plying their trade.

Lucky Dan grinned, calmly withdrew his Colt Walker pistol, raised it, levered back the hammer.

"Gents," he said, "which one of you wants the lead first? It don't make me no never mind—hell, I'm an American. I'm all for equality."

"Dumbass Whiteman," Raccoon Mask replied, "we don' want to fight. We kill you, maybe you kill a couple of us. Not worth it. Don' make no difference what Chief Red Bear said. We ain't in Koyukon lands now, so what he say don't count. This place, the redoubt, it's neutral, that's what. To hell with old grudges. Koyukons, Ingaliks, Aleuts, we all come here some time or another. Other places maybe we fight, not here."

"Goddamn right," Honker agreed. "This place to drink, then hump the womens little bit. Have fun. No damn fightin', that's what the Gossacks say. Go fight somewhere else. Gossacks hokay long as they stay here. Come over to our village, then we stick 'em with arrows. Goddam wild dogs, but here, St. Mike, they give us trade goods for our furs. Pat us on the back, let us get drunk with medicine water. Don' even care what we done at Nulato. . . ."

Locke glanced from Raccoon Mask to Honker to New Spear to Bull's Pizzle—the happy, utterly uncivilized faces, the masks of the wild Alaskan interior.

"I could shoot all four of you bastards. . . ."

"Hey, Luckydan," Bull's Pizzle said, "you hokay. Put gun away. Let's get drunk an' be friends. Maybe later we be enemies again."

"Damn right hokay," New Spear agreed. "Hey, Gossack vodka man, bring us more medicine. We got plenty money. Want to get stupid like Whitemen, then go screw hell out of pay-ladies. They waitin' for us, rub perfume on their titties an' up an' down their legs. They want to mate so much we probably goin' make them pay us!"

"Crazy damn slant-eyed Injuns," a big Creole laughed, "I go with you—show you how to do it, by God! Show you which end to stick it in. The whores, they don't like it in their ears. . . ."

"This Andre Salmon-eye," Raccoon Mask explained, motioning toward the *promyshlenniki*, "half Gossack an' half Ingalik. Don' know which half is worse. He talks a lot, can't even get his plaything to stand up!"

The Koyukons chuckled happily.

"I show you *plaything!*" Andre Salmon-eye said, threatening to unlace his breeches.

"He think he got orca the killer whale, but it's only little minnow out of a brook," Bull's Pizzle said. "Jealous, that's what. He knows why I got my name. Hey, Luckydan, put the gun away, hokay? You come with us. We all have fun tonight."

Locke thrust his pistol back under his belt.

"Sure," he said. "What the hell? Guess I'm not obliged to put the lot of you under for what one particular whipped son of a bitch did in a fit of anger—and he's dead anyhow."

"Damn right," Honker agreed. "You shoot him, just like that, bang. Sent him down Raven Man's tunnel with big hole in 'im. You did what's right. Somebitch does somethin' like that, he gotta expect to get shot. Let's all drink some more, hokay?"

"I show you killer whale," Andre Salmon-eye insisted.

Several flasks of vodka later, Locke and the four Koyukons and Andre were singing songs in three or four languages at once. They pounded one another on the back, engaged in several bouts of wrist-wrestling, a sport unknown either to the Indians or to Andre, but one which Dan was happy to teach. After it was quite clear that no one could defeat the American at his own game, the drinking companions began to challenge one another, with Dan serving as the official referee.

"*Nyet, nyet*, dumb bastards," Andre cried out. "What we wasting all our strength for? Gotta save something for the whores, otherwise they fuck us all to death. Them women ready for humping, I say. They know Andre-the-Whale comin' to visit tonight, by God! Come on, you short peckers—let's go do what the women want us to. . . ."

"You comin' with us, Luckydan?" New Spear asked. "Be good for you. Man needs to have lotsa women, otherwise he dies young."

"Dies young sometimes from havin' too many women," Raccoon Mask laughed. "Hell, I lived long enough anyway."

"Okay, okay," Dan agreed. "Maybe I will at that. I guess the living have to go on living, don't they? Sort of a way of saying good-bye to the damned Youcan River, the way this child sees it. Lead onward, friend New Spear. Andre here, he's so drunk he's sure to pass out before we even get there. . . ."

"Pass out, hell!" Andre Salmon-eye grumbled. "*Shto eh-tah znahcheet*, what does this mean? Maybe a Boston passes out—a Russian-Aleut, he sure as hell don't. Where them spread-leg women?"

Holding one another up, the men staggered from the tavern and lurched their way through the long twilight that passed for night this time of the Arctic year and toward the little whorehouse, where they were less than enthusiastically welcomed by the sleepy women—who had already accomplished their evening's objectives with Russian officers and a few of the *promyshlenniki*. The additional business, however, was not to be turned away.

Two Malemiut women, sisters apparently, took a shine to Lucky Dan, and, with a good deal of whooping and laughing on the part of the Koyukons, he was ushered toward an area partitioned off by means of a gray company blanket fastened to a peeled-pole rafter.

At the last moment, Dan disengaged himself from the two women—apologizing as he did so, claiming that he was simply too exhausted to be making love that night.

"Hell," Andre said, "you don' gotta do nothing, Locke. They do it all for you."

"Can't explain, can't explain," Dan said. "It's not that I wouldn't be proud to lie down with you ladies, it's just that. . . ."

"Just that Loon-cry's still got hold of his manhood an' won't let go of it, that's what," Raccoon Mask said. "He ain't got no spirit for anyone else. Sometime a woman, she gets hold of a man that way. . . ."

Dan felt the blood come to his face. Suddenly he was neither tired nor drunk, or so it seemed. He turned, momentarily considered reaching once more for his Colt Walker.

"Son of a bitch!" he said. "Don't be speaking about . . . the lost one . . . that way. I swear to God, I'll murder the lot of you!"

"Calm down, man," Andre put in. "The dumbass Koyukon, he didn't mean nothin' by it. *Kto?* Who? This Loon-cry,

she's your woman? Hell, we all got women—they don't care
if we do a little screwin' when we're away from 'em."

"You don't understand, Salmon-eye old fellow. My woman
. . . Loon-cry . . . she's dead. These men . . . one of their
tribesmen killed her. . . ."

The Malemiut sisters were once again tugging at Dan, but
he patiently pushed them aside.

"Just ain't up to it, that's all. Okay, no harm done. We're
all drunk as skunks, an' I guess you didn't mean nothing by what
you said. Okay. Raccoon Mask, he's right. Loon-cry's dead, but
I can't lie down with a woman right now. Goddamn it, I've had
this knot in my guts ever since it happened, and I'm no good for
any other woman—maybe I never will be again."

The Koyukon men exchanged glances, and the professional women, realizing they had an emotional problem on
their hands, began to consider the best way to get down to
business, at least with the customers who had no qualms about
what they were doing.

"Shit, Luckydan, you don't gotta worry about that. Guess
you didn't know, huh?" Bull's Pizzle asked.

"Not making sense, not making sense," Dan said. "What
the hell you talking about, you blithering savage?"

Honker laughed.

"No way he could know," he said to his fellow Koyukons.

"Know what, damn it!"

Raccoon Mask began to laugh, slapping at his ample belly
with both hands as he did so.

"Not dead at all," he replied between guffaws.

"Who isn't dead?"

"Your woman, that's who," New Spear said. "Come on,
Luckydan, let's play with the whores. After that we tell you
everything."

"Tell me right now, you heathen sonsabitches, or I'll blow
holes in all of you!"

"Hokay, hokay," Honker said. "I tell you—then I go with
the sisters, give 'em both good ride. Loon-cry, she's got hold
of your manhood I guess, just like Raccoon Mask says. She
ain't dead. Got stabbed an' bled a lot, but she didn't go off
with old Raven Man; no sir. Hell, she's back in Red Bear's
village—keeps thinkin' you goin' return to her, bring little one
along. . . ."

11

Return to Red Bear's Village

New Spear gestured with both hands, at the same time winking at the Creole woman who stood grinning beside him.

"The women, they harder to kill than men. Used to bleedin' all time anyway. Got more practice. Hey, Luckydan, your wife, she ain't even hurt none. Little scar, maybe, that's all. Chief Red Bear, he called old Crazy Goose the medicine woman, she's damn good doctor, knows how to cure pains and suck out spirits. Crazy Goose goes into trance an' wanders off toward the Spirit World until she finds Loon-cry an' brings her back."

Bull's Pizzle nodded.

"You gone, an' Red Bear tells Loon-cry you ain't never coming back. She still don' want nothin' to do with any of the men—not even Red Bear himself. He wants to have her as third wife. Others gettin' too old, maybe. But Loon-cry won't lie down with him."

"You lying heathen bastards! That's not possible!"

"Is possible, all right," New Spear laughed. "Only you better not go back there, Danlock. Red Bear break your back and then cut you open and pull out your guts, spread 'em all around. . . ."

"Aw, shit, Dan," Andre Salmon-eye said, "don' listen to no dumb Injuns. What the hell they know? Come on, Yengee, these whores, they hotter'n hell. . . ."

But before Andre finished speaking Locke was out through the doorway.

Already the sky was beginning to turn blue.

* * *

On shank's mare, he set out along the overland Koyukon
Trail toward Nulato. A one-man assault on Red Bear's village,
he knew well enough, would be nothing more than a form
of suicide—and no doubt a suicide of the most unpleasant
sort. On the other hand, if Loon-cry really were alive. . . .
As it was, what good was life to him? The North Country
had in fact long since become his home—he'd entered into
some kind of pact with the great, sprawling, nearly trackless
land, and a prospect of heading south to the States made
sense only if he knew positively that the woman he'd chosen
for a mate and who had inexplicably chosen him as well and
who had borne him a child—that Loon-cry was dead. But
now. . . .

If the Koyukons were lying, he resolved, one way or another he'd put all of them under. To bring wild hope back to
life in a man who, deep inside, had been little more than
sleepwalking, a dead man fated to stumble about a few more
years—to do such a thing as some kind of insane and drunken
jest. . . . A simple bullet in the brain for each of them would
hardly be ample justice.

But if Loon-cry were actually alive—then, one way or
another, not even Red Bear and all his bloodthirsty damned
warriors were going to stop Lucky Dan Locke, not so long as
an ounce of life remained in him.

Northeast along the sound he strode, moving ahead
like a man possessed, one who was suddenly stronger and
more certain of his purpose than he'd ever been in his life
before—except possibly on the day when he'd entered the
Kutchin village intent upon exacting revenge against Raven's
Egg but even then not necessarily determined to kill the
man. It had not been a time for the exercise of common sense
but rather a time for action, and the same was true of the
present.

Light glittered off across the gray-green water, and swarms
of gulls shrieked and drifted away overhead. Half a dozen polar
bears shambled along in an irregular line by the water's edge,
almost like some strange parade in yellow-white fur, and Dan
muttered greetings to the huge beasts, at the same time check-
ing the load in his cap-and-ball Hawken and moving off upslope
away from the sand and gravel littoral, taking an alternate route

among gorse sedges and across a long, rounded hilltop where Arctic poppies and crimson fireweed were growing in profusion.

The white bears were, if anything, even more dangerous than the grizzlies—and there was no point in courting unnecessary danger.

A few miles further along, once again on the main trail close by the water's edge, Dan passed by a series of flat-topped rock ledges emergent from the restless sea and seeming almost to be floating upon it. And, from a distance, the rocks seemed to be moving. Then he detected the gruntings, barkings, and moanings of seals and sea lions.

By noon of the second day, he had reached the Eskimo village of Unalakleet where, as he'd been told in Kaltag and Nulato, the Koyukon Trail reached the sea.

Upstream then along the big creek that rushed down through tundra out of a sprawl of sparsely timbered ridges that rose gradually toward Debauch Mountain at the crest of the little coastward range, its rounded summit white and bare and gleaming with snowfields even at midsummer.

The sun circled northwestward, imperceptibly dipping toward the horizon. Locke struggled ahead, but now each step was an effort as his entire body cried out for rest.

A waterfall thundered over a sheer gray-black stoneface, and below a pool from whose surface gray mists rose in the gaining twilight was a sedgy area of bunchgrass and stunted willows.

Dan stumbled down toward the clearing, slipped, fell— at the same time clinging to his rifle so that the weapon would not be damaged by striking against the slippery, rounded stones he'd been attempting to descend. He slid all the way to the bottom of the slope, lay there a moment, Hawken held over his head, and attempted to assess the damage. His right ankle throbbed, but he could still move it—and no sensation of pain such as might come from splintered bones. He'd taken a terrific jolt in his left shoulder, but when he sat up he realized that he still had full mobility of his limb.

He cursed silently for a long moment and then slowly rose to his feet. His free hand had been badly bruised, but he was able to flex the fingers.

"Goddamn clumsy Yank!" he muttered. "Got to stay in one piece if you want to have any chance at all of getting Loon-cry away from the Koyukons. . . ."

From beyond the pool came a dull thudding of falling water, and mists spiraled upward, vanishing in a luminous gray of twilight. On the pool's surface were four Canadian geese—nearly motionless, as though in contemplation of the human creature who'd come sprawling down into their world.

"All right," Lucky Dan laughed. "So this child ain't the most graceful bastard alive. One remark out of you four, and by Gawd I'll have the lot of you for dinner."

The geese considered Locke's invitation for a brief moment, and then they glided off, putting another two or three yards between themselves and the human, deciding, perhaps, that an extra margin of safety was called for.

No swarm of mosquitoes about. That, at least, was a good sign—for the damned insects could, at times, so plague a man that he was pushed to the very edge of insanity. Dan recalled the tale of one H.B.C. trapper over on Copper River who had been bitten so badly that he apparently took his own life. . . .

He gathered twigs and broke off a thick section of dead willow. Within a short time he had a good fire burning, and he even took time before sleeping to brew up a pan full of coffee. He chewed at mouthfuls of jerky, sipped hot, bitter coffee, and stared at the faintly visible movements of the water-fall.

Various faces appeared in the rising mists, faded, re-formed, faded once more.

He heard the geese, no longer visible at all from where he was sitting, enter into a brief disagreement among themselves, complete with a faint flapping of wings, and then go still once more.

The utter isolation, the strange, fierce, lonely beauty of this land—and now the new possibility that Loon-cry might miraculously be alive: how that had indeed brought everything else back to life and, yes, Lucky Dan Locke as well.

At length, heaping whatever driftwood he'd been able to scrounge up onto the fire and breathing in deeply of the chill air of midsummer, he pulled a sewn-hareskin blanket Loon-

cry had made for him over his shoulders, leaned back against
a worn shelf of stone, and slept.

Dreamed.

*Men crowded around the table, and all the chits were up
for grabs. Hans Larsson was standing behind him, methodi-
cally pounding him on the back. Not dead, then? A mistake?
My God, he'd buried a man who wasn't ready to go tramping
off among the stars. . . .*

*Jashue, hur står det till? Hur mycket, Dan, how much
are you betting? Yarg har gått vilse, I am lost. . . .*

*He turned to stare at Hans, as if unable to believe the
man was actually there.*

*Hans, yes, but not Hans at all—instead a man in trapper's
clothing, but the face was a mask: wide, staring eyes, green
irises surrounded by yellow, nose and mouth the color of cured
salmon flesh, one half of the face detailed in red, the other in
black, and a complete halo of black all around it, a halo of
raven feathers. . . .*

Den är stängd, Dan, the door, ja, it is open. Step through!

*Talk English, Hans, you thick-skulled son of a bitch, and
take off the damned funny face, it's probably been soaking in
Koyukon medicine for a goddamn century. . . .*

*Let's see your cards, Daniel Locke. It kills me, playing
with you amateurs—only a game, only a game!*

*Mike McLafferty. Fringed black jacket and Spanish som-
brero. Blue-eyed card thief smoking a cigar, biting down on
the tobacco and grinning as though he hadn't a worry in the
world.*

*Turn 'em up, Locke. I can't wait forever. Tell ye, I'm
heading downriver tomorrow—goin' to buy a damn big brick
house and marry a proper woman. Best you be thinking about
something of the sort yourself, Daniel. We can't spend our
whole lives wandering around the mountains. Esnaih, hell.
That's just being rootless is all. Let's see what you got.*

*You turn 'em up first, Big Mike. Give me a chance to think
about what it is I want to do. . . .*

*Don't even know how to play poker, for Gawd's sake.
Takin' candy from children. I've already called you—the game's
up. . . .*

What's in my hand? I haven't even looked yet. . . .

*Hans Larsson reached down, forced him to turn the cards,
one at a time.*

*A pair of trays, nothing more—but inexplicably the cards
were both hearts.*

*The men standing about the table began to grumble.
Cheating—and can't even do that right. . . .*

*Big Mike McLafferty stood up, adjusted his sombrero,
grinned.*

*It beats me, Daniel. Hell, a full house ain't no match for
ye. . . . Guess I'll be ridin' for St. Louis.*

*Then Locke was alone somewhere in a vast, snow-covered
landscape, only the table was still there. McLafferty's cards
were still on the table, face down. Dan reached across, turned
them up, was hardly able to believe his eyes. The faces—all
printed with ravens, the birds wings-out, beaked heads limp
to one side and crowned with wreaths of thorns.*

Crucified. . . .

He awoke, stumbled groggily to the water, splashed cold-
ness over his face, glanced up immediately as a fanning of wings
went over his head. The geese, perhaps startled at the human's
movements, had taken to the air.

"Go in peace!" he shouted after them and then returned
to the still-smoking remains of his campfire.

Warmed-over coffee, a chunk of hard bread, and a few
mouthfuls of jerked caribou flesh: he was once more ready for
the trail. Locke shouldered his pack, picked up his Hawken,
and climbed back to the path he'd been following before exhaustion called him down.

The momentary outline of a human visage in mists rising
from beneath the hurtling waters of the fall: that son of a bitch
Red Bear. . . .

Locke shrugged and directed himself upstream toward the
south shoulder of Debauch Mountain, not visible from here
along the creek, but its presence felt—yes, like a barrier, a
great stone that lay between him and his purpose.

Two more long days of walking—the little river growing
smaller, then no more than a rivulet, then nothing at all. He
stood astride a long ridge and gazed eastward into the broad
taiga basin of the Kuikpak, Old Lot of Water, the Youcan.
Faint, so faint it could hardly be discerned at all, smoke was

drifting upward from two sources perhaps thirty or so miles apart.

"Kaltag and Nulato," he said aloud.

He headed for Nulato.

Lucky Dan was welcomed into the kashim by Black Claw and Salmon Berry, the Yukon woman serving him a tightly woven basket full of stew and hovering about as the two men talked.

"You still alive, eh?" Black Claw asked.

"More or less, old friend. But what's a hell of a lot more to the point, and that's the reason I'm back here," Dan managed between mouthfuls of the hot, thick porridge, "Loon-cry's still alive. She's alive, I tell you."

Black Claw and Salmon Berry glanced at one another, concern showing in their faces.

"Maybe you rest little bit first," Salmon Berry said, "then tell us story. Your yeg—maybe he wandering in dream place while you still awake. Loon-cry gone to other land. You saw it happen, you don't remember, Luckydan?"

Dan shook his head impatiently.

"I'm not losing my mind, Salmon Berry. My yeg's fine—in better shape now than it's been for months. She's alive—or at least she may be. Four of Red Bear's men at St. Mike—I got drunk with 'em, and they let it slip. Red Bear's got her, wants her to be one of his wives."

The scar-faced Kutchin shook his head.

"Whitemen very stupid," Black Claw replied. "You saw her killed, Dan Locke—that is what you said. A Koyukon warrior knifed her to death after you defeated him. . . ."

Dan nodded.

"Yes, that's what I thought. But . . . the Koyukons say she survived and is now well. They wouldn't let me take her body, I told you. Wouldn't even let me see her. Maybe that bastard Red Bear knew all along. . . ."

"Is this possible? Now you wish Black Claw to help you? My debt was to Loon-cry, not to you. This some kind of trick, eh? I should have murdered you as soon as I was free of my debt. . . ."

"I killed your son, Black Claw, but he gave me no choice. He'd gone crazy, just as you've admitted. Loon-cry saved your life. Here's your chance to pay off that debt you used to grouse about all the time. Well, we're friends now, the way I see it. If you don't want to go with me, I won't force you, you old thief. Now that I think about it, you'd probably just get in my way, anyhow. . . ."

"Don't want Black Claw to go to Red Bear's village," Salmon Berry said. "Don't want you to go either, Luckydan. Both of you end up dead, that's what. Them Koyukons, they our cousins, but we don't trust 'em. Nobody trusts Red Bear. Those men, Luckydan, they tell you big story so you go back to Red Bear's village. Want you dead, that's all. I love Loon-cry like daughter, but she in other world now. Is time to let her spirit go."

"Makes sense," Dan agreed. "But I have to go there all the same. Don't think they meant to tell me—I've got a strange, haunting feeling they spoke the truth."

"Dumb bastard Whiteman. Get both of us cut up, all right. Shit. Hokay, hokay. Two of us take on whole damned Koyukon village, eh? Hokay. Hokay, by God, we do 'er. You got good death song ready, Luckydan? Little bit luck left? Dumb as a British, even if you ain't. Bostons even stupider than bloody British. Hokay. Maybe we ought to go back up Lot of Water to get Otter Pipe send Kutchin warriors after Red Bear, Broken Antler too, maybe few Brit trappers. Then we got chance."

Locke finished the last of his stew, placed his empty basket on the floor of the kashim. He stared into the coals of the firepit.

"Always heard Black Claw was a brave man," he said. "But I guess those stories about fighting the Hans and Tutchones —just wild tales . . . ? All right, then. I'll go by myself. Truth to say, I don't blame you—and I'm not even sure there's a chance in hell. Have to try it, though. Challenge Red Bear, head to head."

"Dumbass sonabitch. Hokay, I go with you. See what Raven Man's mother-in-law likes to do in her lodge. You got money, Luckydan. You leave it for Salmon Berry? Then I go. Save Loon-cry, bring 'er back from spirit world, rassle Raven Man for 'er, by God, if Red Bear ain't got 'er an' damned Koyukons lied about her still bein' alive. After that I'm free to stick a knife in you."

Locke grinned.

"That ought to please Loon-cry," he said, "if she's really alive."

Dan acquired a canoe and additional ammunition from Ivan Pavloff, the Creole trader at the newly reopened Russian-American post. He also bought a number of blankets, half a dozen steel-bladed skinning knives, some traps, some rope, and a quantity of needles, pots, and other household implements—hoping once again to be able to buy Loon-cry back from Red Bear or at least to settle down the Koyukon chief's no doubt ruffled fur.

The remainder of his money he gave to Salmon Berry, as Black Claw had insisted.

"Don' want damn money," the woman scowled. "Men got no sense. You bring my ugly ol' man back to me, Luckydan. Then we be friends again. You get Black Claw killed, maybe I stick knife in you myself."

"I understand how you feel, Salmon, damned if I don't. I wish there was a better way. I can promise you this much —if Black Claw don't come back, it'll be because Red Bear put me under too."

"Never mind 'bout that. Just bring 'im back."

"Shut up, woman. Black Claw can take care of self, hokay," the scar-faced one grumbled.

Salmon Berry responded to Black Claw's harsh words by pulling him into her arms and hugging him tightly. Then she released the old warrior and embraced Dan as well.

"Men gotta do crazy things, I guess. You bring Loon-cry, both of you, back safe to Salmon Berry, hokay?"

Having completed their transactions in Nulato, Locke and Black Claw set out up the river, proceeding the twenty-five miles to the mouth of the Koyukuk River and turning upstream along this tributary, continuing two or three miles before making camp for the night.

The barred hawk owls were crying, perhaps half a dozen of them back in the taiga away from the river—vibrant, penetrating bursts of hollow sound. Far away, eastward across the Koyukuk, wolves were singing, their cries drifting on the wind and seeming one with the air itself.

"Two packs meeting," Black Claw remarked, "old friends gettin' together. Or maybe they telling each other about which way the caribou moving."

"Heard it before," Lucky Dan nodded. "Be good if human varmints could get along as well as the wolves. Just a matter of sticking to different territories, that's probably the secret to it. Like the Russians and the British here in Alaska—so long as one's upriver and the other's downriver, everything's just fine."

"Goddamn Russians bring their God with 'em. Ought to leave that one at home—or else stay at home themselves, wherever they come from. Hudson Bay men, at least they ain't brought no God along, not yet anyway. Russians and Hudson Bay, they like cousins. That right? Only both want furs, so they come to Lot of Water to get 'em. Maybe better if both go home. Boston too."

Lucky Dan stared across the campfire at his companion.

"Meaning me. But where the hell is my home, Black Claw? You meet up with a woman, and by God she starts meaning everything to you. You want her to come with you, but if she does, then she's not at home. Home's a hard place to put your finger on."

Black Claw mused for a moment.

"Guess I want go back to Porcupine River. Miss my Kutchin wife—good old girl. My son, Broken Antler. Also dumbass Otter Pipe, even if he does think being friends with Murray and Stewart, that's a good idea. Miss Raven's Egg, too, only I can't go visit him no more."

A long silence ensued. The two men had difficulty looking at one another.

"I'm sorry. . . ," Lucky Dan muttered.

Black Claw nodded.

"Getting old," he said. "Used to be big warrior—crazy bastard in those days. Liked to fight—liked danger. Now I don' know. Sleep for a while I guess. . . ."

The Kutchin drew his bearskin robe about him and within a few minutes was snoring regularly.

And off in the taiga, the hawk owls continued to hoot. But the wolves had grown silent.

Dan rose, strode down to the river's bank, stared upstream through the thin gray summer twilight, and began to wrestle once again with the implications of what Honker, Raccoon Mask, New Spear, and Bull's Pizzle had told him. Had they spoken the truth—or was the whole thing simply a means of getting him to go to bed with the Malemiut sisters—or was the whole thing, as Black Claw suggested, a sort of spur of the moment makeshift joke or scheme to get him to make an attempt to rescue the long-dead Loon-cry? Nothing made much sense. Had he not himself seen her fall, her blood spill? An image that had haunted his dreams ever since. . . .

Locke listened for a while longer to the intertwined sounds of the owls and the movement of Koyukuk water. Then he turned back to the campfire, lay down, pulled his blanket about him, and slept.

When he awoke, Black Claw was standing above him. The scar-faced Kutchin had a knife in his hand.

"Be easy to kill you whenever I want, eh?" Black Claw grinned. "Don' worry. Just cuttin' splinters to get fire going. You got coffee in the pack, Luckydan?"

The scheme Locke and Black Claw had devised involved making an open approach to Red Bear's village—to come in peace, bearing gifts. The tactic just might work—or so the two men convinced themselves.

"Seems like you try this before, Luckydan," Black Claw said of the plan. "Didn't work worth a damn then. Why you think it work now?"

"Just can't seem to come up with anything else. You got something better in mind?"

"Sneak in at night, cut all their throats? Probably somebody wake up, kill us, hokay, but we take them with us to Raven Man's mother-in-law. Other way they just gonna kill us anyway, take all your things, they not have any trouble."

"I got a curious feelin' Red Bear don't work that way. I'm beginning to think the bastard's even got some sense of fair play. Not sure why I believe it except that he's had the chance to kill me outright twice and he hasn't done it."

"Hokay, damned sneakin' Koyukon your brother after all. We do it your way. I'm gettin' too old to worry about dying anyway. Maybe Salmon Berry miss me, though. Hope she be miserable when Black Claw is dead."

* * *

A few miles downstream from the Koyukon encampment, they realized they'd been sighted, but since the only option lay in turning tail and fleeing back down Koyukuk River and trying to figure out some alternate scheme, Locke and Black Claw determined to press ahead.

To their surprise, no welcoming committee waited for them at the landing area below the village. Indeed, no one seemed to be present at all.

"Somethin' wrong, hokay," Black Claw said. "Damn sure they knew we comin'. What you think, Luckydan?"

"Maybe we figured wrong. Well, keep your eyes peeled, Black Claw."

"Only got one good one," the old Kutchin warrior grumbled. "Works pretty hokay, though. Don't think maybe we get back in our canoe an' get the hell out of here? You good at runnin' down river, Dan. Maybe we try that right now?"

"Grab a pack of trade goods, old friend. If Red Bear's men aren't shooting arrows at us now, then perhaps they're not going to. . . ."

Loaded down, the two men made their way up from the landing area and entered into the central portion of the village.

Still no one in sight.

Then the Koyukons appeared all at once. Their faces were painted, and each man was armed either with bow or with spear, while a few held fusees.

At this point Chief Red Bear stepped forward, approaching Locke and Black Claw.

"Luckydan," the Koyukon said in a deep voice, "you come to wrong place. Drop your guns and knives, and I tell my men not kill you on the spot. Why you come back here? Not hear what I told you before?"

"I have brought the chief some gifts," Dan replied.

"I take these things. Maybe one or two other things as well."

Dan and Black Claw did as they were bidden and then stepped back a couple of paces.

"Where's Loon-cry?" Locke called out. "I have been told that my woman is still alive—that she's here in your village. . . ."

But then the Koyukon warriors pressed forward, and within moments Dan and Black Claw had been bound and marched across the circular area at village center, pushed down into an empty underground lodge, the entryway sealed shut behind them.

After a long interval of silence, Black Claw cleared his throat.

"Damn! We still alive, anyway," he said.

"For a little while, at least. But I'm afraid the fat's in the fire now."

"Neither one of us very smart, crazy Boston."

"That's what Loon-cry told me a long time ago. Could be she was right. If it's worth anything, I'm sorry I got you into this."

Another long silence, and then Black Claw spoke from the darkness again.

"You think they really done that?" he asked.

"What are you talking about?"

"Roasted Bulegin the Russian, ate him for dinner."

12

I Have Come for My Woman

Time passed with killing slowness within the damp, dark confines of the kashim—largely because of the utter uncertainty of what was to come next—or was it the fear of their altogether too likely doom? In any case, reflections upon the grotesque fate that apparently had overtaken Bulegin crossed their minds.

"Don't like being shut in," Black Claw complained. "Bastard Koyukons don't even feed us. What they think we are, anyway? I kill two, three of 'em if I get a chance."

Dan laughed.

"You just haven't had enough experience, my friend. In Nulato—sometimes the Gawdamned Russkies just sort of forgot to bring me my rations, though I shouldn't be speaking ill of the dead. Deriabin was a decent enough sort, as it turned out. In this particular case, however, I have to admit that I'm not all that eager to get let out. I think Red Bear may be planning something relatively unpleasant for me. With a bit of luck, old friend, the Koyukon honcho will see the wisdom of letting you go—get right down to it, he has no quarrel with you. In any case, I'm sorry I got you into this mess. Things don't seem to be turning out the way I hoped they would."

"I tell Red Bear that Otter Pipe and the Kutchin warriors come pay him a visit, by God, if he don't let us go. That ain't much bluff, I guess. Hokay. Maybe we still get out of this. If Loon-cry really alive an' Red Bear likes her, then he's gonna listen to her. She going tell him to let us go on back down Koyukon River. . . ."

Locke made a growling sound, stood up, and gave a hefty push against the peeled-spruce beams overhead. But even if there were a way out through the top, he realized, very little could be accomplished—at least until nearly everyone in the village was sleeping.

"Probably no more than a couple of guards keeping watch tonight. Black Claw, old companyero, we might have a chance if we could break through without waking everyone in the encampment. But yes, I gather your point. Loon-cry convinces the chief to let us go, and in exchange she'll marry the no-neck son of a bitch, right? Because that's what my Koyukon friends in St. Mike told me—the big cheese wants her, and she's been resisting him. So maybe it'll be our freedom in exchange for Loon-cry bedding the toad-sucking coyote. Guess my luck's about run out. Couldn't last forever, I suppose. In the long run, fate's impartial as hell. I had a dream on the way across from Unalakleet—I was gambling, not the hand game, and my opponent's cards all had Raven Man on them. Death. But he just walked away from the table and left me sitting there with all the chips. So. But dreams are usually different than life."

Black Claw shrugged.

"Some dreams tell truth, some don't. Some dreams just how we wish things to be—but mebbe Raven Man tellin' you something. Luckydan. Hokay. Loon-cry's good woman, even if I didn't think so long time ago when Raven's Egg want to marry her even though she was an orphan. She'll do what gotta be. We tried the only way we could—just didn't work out, that's all. I don' know. Could be worse for her than bein' one of the head chief's women—she'll be favorite for little while, anyway. Maybe Koyukons hold you captive, wait for me to go to Ikogmut to get Walks-Between-Worlds, your little one. That be part of the deal."

"If it comes down to it, I suppose my daughter's better off with her mother—if Loon-cry's alive at all. But I don't think I can live with it, Black Claw, nor die with it either—not unless I believed it was what Loon-cry really wanted. No, damn it, I've got to have my wife back. I want to be with her, even if I have to die in order to get to her. Does that make any sense? Coming back here was a fool's errand, all right. I saw her die, damn it, and I know I'm just grabbing at straws in the wind. Jesus Christ, this whole thing's like a crazy damned dream. Shit, Black Claw, maybe we all drowned coming down the Youcan. Maybe we're dead already and have just been dreaming everything that's happened since then. Hell's a nightmare that never ends."

Black Claw toyed with the concept a moment.

"You in my death-dream, Luckydan, or me in yours? Anyhow, ain't no such thing as hell. That's crazy stuff Russian priests use to frighten old women."

"Bring food, you Koyukon sonabitches!" Black Claw yelled. "Gonna Goddam starve us to death? I'm Kutchin war chief—demand talking to Red Bear! Hey, whatsamatter with you guards, you asleep?"

"Not going to do any good that way," Locke said. "Patience, old friend."

"Koyukons eat moose shit!" Black Claw persisted. "Goddam afraid to fight me—coward skunks!"

Locke was on his feet now, waiting.

"Wives suck caribou cocks, by damn. Stick greasy pieces of wood into cunts because Koyukon men ain't got nothin' to fill 'em up!"

"You're going to get us killed ahead of schedule. What . . . ?"

"Listen, Luckydan," Black Claw whispered. "Ain't no sounds at all. Ain't no guards out there, that's why. Let's get hell out of here!"

"Worth a chance, I guess."

The two men, joining efforts in the near darkness of the kashim, threw their combined weight against the entryway— once, twice, a third time. Then the makeshift brace against the doorway snapped, and Black Claw and Lucky Dan were through the entry.

A few stars glowed in the thin darkness of Arctic summer night, and the central grounds of the Koyukon village were indeed empty.

"What the hell do you make of this?" Lucky Dan asked.

"Don' know. Almost like Red Bear wanted us to get away—maybe track us down an' then kill us. Only why he want to do that?"

"No time for theories, Scarface old man. Let's see if they left us a canoe. . . ."

The two moved carefully, keeping to shadows as best they could, and proceeded to the landing area below the village.

Their canoe was precisely where they'd left it. More than that, their weapons were stowed aboard.

"Son of a bitch! Red Bear left us unguarded precisely so that we could make an escape. The only way any of this could make sense is if Loon-cry really is alive. . . ."

"Let's get hell out of here, Luckydan. Once we out on river, no way they going to catch us again."

"Ammunition's here too," Dan said. "And no doubt clear paddling all the way back down Koyukon River. He doesn't want us dead—he wants us out of here."

"By God, Black Claw agrees with 'im. You damn fool to come here in first place, me even bigger damn fool to come here with you, no matter what. Let's go, Luckydan!"

Locke turned, stared back uphill toward the village. A hint of movement in the shadows? Several men, almost certainly, watching to see what would happen next.

Dan reached for his Hawken and the ammunition belt on which his Colt Walker and his Bowie knife were sheathed, buckled that about his waist.

"I'm staying," he said. "I've got no real reason to live without Loon-cry, and I'm not going to turn tail now. Black Claw, you head downriver. You've got a wife . . . no, two wives . . . to tend to. If Loon-cry and I don't show up in Nulato within two weeks, say, I want you to find Father Georgi and Snow Flower at Ikogmut—take little Naomi back to Fort You-can. She's yours to raise as your own. I think Loon-cry would approve of that. Don't argue with me, damn it. Get in the canoe and shove off—or by God I'll blow a hole in you right now. Someone's got to look out for my daughter. . . ."

"Luckydan, you gone crazy. Nahoens must of stole your *yeg* while we was in jail kashim. If you stay, then Black Claw stay."

Locke thumbed back the hammer on his Colt Walker. The sharp metallic click, in the midst of nighttime silence, had a distinctly ominous sound.

"Hokay, hokay, crazy sonamabitch Whiteman. Never did have any sense. . . ."

In the next moment Black Claw was into the canoe, nearly capsizing it in the process, and the craft went knifing silently out into the dark waters. Dan Locke stood watching until he could no longer detect movement on the river, and then he turned and began to walk back uphill toward the Koyukon village.

The sun hung well above the horizon when the first Ko-yukons arose, some of them intent on walking to the river for a morning swim, when they became aware that a small fire was burning in the big firepit at the center of the village. The strange, bearded Whiteman, presumed captured the previous night, was now sitting there nonchalantly—as though he had every right in the world to do so and furthermore made serious pretensions to having good sense.

The Koyukons were puzzled—both those who assumed the Whiteman and his Kutchin companion had been shut into the empty kashim and also those who'd had the privilege of Red Bear's confidence and so had every reason to suppose they'd seen the last of Daniel Locke the Boston man.

The trapper's Kutchin companion was nowhere about, so he, at least, had demonstrated common wisdom and had doubt-less escaped down the river. As for the Whiteman who was neither Gossack nor Anglois but who'd first come to the village during the time of the spring moon and had slain Blue Weasel after defeating him in combat, that one was clearly possessed by some spirit of madness—indeed, was all but forcing Red Bear now to have him put to death.

Most of the Koyukons gave the bearded one by the fire a wide berth and went about their morning business, though others made their way directly to Red Bear's lodge to alert the chief.

An hour or more passed, and still the Koyukon leader made no appearance. And still the Whiteman, now pacing slowly back and forth, remained at the center of the village.

It was difficult to ignore him, but the Koyukons did their best.

Then the Yengee began to fire his pistol into the air.

Lucky Dan slipped the spare cylinder into his Colt Walker and stood idly reloading the one he'd removed.

"*Giyeg*," one man muttered as he walked stiffly past. "Death spirit. . . ."

Dan grinned, winked at the man, noted that the Koyukon turned his head quickly in the other direction. Then Locke raised his Hawken to his shoulder, drew aim on a drying rack laden with caribou flesh, and fired—the fifty-five caliber shot thundering over the mounded tops of the kashims.

He'd just finished reloading and thrusting his wiping stick back into place when Red Bear appeared. The chief's face was painted with daubed circles of red and black, very much like the image in Dan's dream, and clusters of raven feathers dangled from either ear. The chief was stripped to the waist, his corded muscles glistening from bear grease that had been liberally applied.

"Luckydan, why you still here?" Red Bear demanded.

"I've come for my woman, Loon-cry. She's here, Gawddamn it, and she's alive. A fish eagle appeared to me in a vision and told me the truth."

"You are indeed a brave man, Daniel Locke. Perhaps I should kill you long ago, that time when you buried your friend. I spare you that day because I respect what you did. Look. Your woman is dead—you saw her fall, saw her bleeding. . . ."

"Fish Eagle says you summoned the shaman Crazy Goose, and she went out into the darkness to bring Loon-cry's spirit back from Raven Man's lodge."

"This eagle speaks strangely, then. What else does the bird tell you, Luckydan?"

"It tells me that the chief of the Koyukons wishes my woman to be one of his wives—and that Loon-cry has turned her face away from him."

"Some wonderful bird, this being from your vision. I tell you what your fate be if you ever return to my village. Even after that I give you chance to escape. You not brave. Stupid, that's what. Now your life ends."

Dan leveled his pistol directly at the chief of the Koyukons.

"Not yet, old fellow. I've come for my woman, and I damn well mean to have her. You say Loon-cry is dead, but you speak crooked words. It was no damned fish eagle that spoke to me. Your own men got drunk and told me what happened—Honker, Bull's Pizzle, New Spear, and Raccoon Mask. You know the gents, eh? We did a little drinkin' together at Redoubt St. Michael. Tell your warriors to bring Loon-cry out where I can see her—either that or I drop you where ye stand."

Still Red Bear hesitated.

"Where your Kutchin friend go, Luckydan? Run away and left you behind?"

"Downriver to Nulato. This quarrel's between you and me, Red Bear. Forget about Black Claw."

The chief nodded and then raised one hand in signal to his men.

"Loon-cry's alive, that's true. But she wishes to stay here among the Koyukons—not go back to White devil who deserts her and child when he gets tired of her. Now I order my warriors to stick an arrow into you from behind, Luckydan."

"And by Gawd I'll blast you to hell at the same time. . . . If Loon-cry wishes to remain here, then I'll go away and never come back, even though I don't wish to live without her. But I want to hear this thing from her own lips, Red Bear. Let me see her, at least, before I die. I must tell her where our child is."

* * *

What happened next came in a blur of suddenness.

Loon-cry was brought forward. Then she saw Dan and cried out, "Danl-ock!" She shook free of the two Koyukons who were apparently her escorts and bolted forward, ran to where Locke was standing, and threw herself into his arms.

"Loon-cry! My God, it's you! I thought you were dead . . . Naomi's with Snow Flower and a priest named Father Georgi, downriver at Ikogmut . . . Snow Flower's taking care of her, she's fine . . . then I met some of Red Bear's men, and they told me . . ."

"Take me away from here, Danl-ock. Naomi Walks-Between-World's all right? Let's go where she is, after that I don't care where we go. Maybe that big river place you tell me about. . . ."

A voice cried out: "Goddam, watch it, Luckydan!"

Then a pistol shot, and Dan spun about, attempting to protect Loon-cry with his own body.

But darkness intervened—a blow to the side of his head, and Locke stumbled forward, struggling to hold onto consciousness.

Pistol, where's my pistol . . . ?

Black Claw, was that his voice?

But unconsciousness won.

Then he was back in the kashim, and Black Claw was with him. Dan rubbed the side of his head. Blood matted in his hair, and pain throbbed behind his eyes.

"What in hell you doing here? Dumbass Kutchin, you're supposed to be halfway to Nulato by now."

"Figure you need help, so I hide canoe an' walk back up river. Didn't help much, though. Red Bear, he had two guys sneakin' up on you. Anyhow, Loon-cry's alive, so I still gotta be her slave for awhile. Think to myself—if I can get 'em free, then it's hokay for me to take revenge for Raven's Egg. Only guess I don' care about that any more. Mebbe you run out of luck now, eh? Goddam, we not very smart, Luckydan. What we gonna do now? Think Loon-cry can save our asses?"

"Doubtful as hell, old friend. I've got a distinct feeling that our spring's run dry, just like you say. Something's going on out there right now—sounds like the Koyukons are getting ready for a celebration, and I suppose we'll be their guests of honor."

Somewhere near to midday the entryway was thrown open and two baskets laden with cold salmon cakes were thrust inside. The bearer of the food, Lucky Dan noted, was one of his erstwhile drinking buddies, Honker.

"Should have gone to bed with Malemiut women," the Koyukon said. "Now bad thing going to happen. We can't do nothing but watch."

"You boys made a quick trip back from the Redoubt— must have been on my trail all the while. Well, situations change, Honker old friend. When the raven squawks, he squawks. No hard feelings. . . ."

Then the entryway was closed once more.

"One them Koyukons you meet at St. Michael?" Black Claw asked.

"Yep."

"Think they help us?"

"Don't know, don't know. I guess we'll accept whatever help's forthcoming, though. Hell, Chief Scarface, we ain't done yet."

"Call me that again, I kill you myself. What you thinkin', Luckydan?"

"Red Bear. The man's full of pride—gets puffed up like a spruce grouse with mating on his mind. We need to touch that pride, one on one. Then maybe. . . ."

"Ain't much," Black Claw replied. "First place, that son-amabitch strong as Goddam bear. You don' wanta wrestle with that one."

"That's a thought. Not a bad idea. Hell, it's not like I've got much to lose," Dan laughed.

"Good point. Hokay. Me, I could beat 'im when I was young. Ain't young no more, though."

The men lapsed into silence, ate the food that had been offered them, and waited for the inevitable.

At length the entryway was thrown open once again, and Black Claw and Dan Locke were escorted to the center of the village, where a pile of brush and driftwood was ablaze. It took no great deal of intuition for the two captives to realize the

Koyukons meant to burn them alive—and possibly chew on their bones afterward.

Red Bear stood before them, his thick arms crossed and his face and chest painted even more elaborately than before. Indeed, his appearance was that of one who was hardly human at all—instead that of some being out of the realm of myth, perhaps one of the ghostly boatmen who were said to take the souls of the dead from Raven Man's lodge and convey them across the Spirit-Lot-of-Water into the Land Beyond.

"New paint job?" Locke grinned. "You're the same old fraud you've always been. I demand that you return my woman to me, Red Bear. You want Loon-cry, but she doesn't want you. What sort of man would suppose he could put a woman's husband to death and then take her to bed? Not even your own warriors could respect such actions."

"This fire burning for you, Daniel Locke. You talk big, but not for long."

"You some chief," Black Claw said. "Me, I am warrior chief of Kutchins. This woman, Loon-cry, was wife to my son. She saves my life, so I owe her a debt. Luckydan, he kills my son. I wish to take Loon-cry back to her little daughter, then my debt paid. After that I kill Luckydan myself. Send your men away, Red Bear, and I kill you too—even without a weapon. Koyukons are weak. They have no heart. Fall down in front of real warrior."

Murmurs of laughter from among the Koyukons.

Red Bear grinned, his teeth glinting with firelight in the rising mists of late twilight.

"You wish to fight me, old man?" Red Bear asked. "Only one good eye—other one probably half blind too. Sure you can see me?"

"The great chief of the Koyukons must give Black Claw his freedom," Dan shouted. "This is my fight, not his. I challenge you to wrestle. If I win, Loon-cry comes with me. Just as I earlier defeated Blue Weasel, so I will now defeat his leader. Do you dare to deny me my challenge, Red Bear?"

The Koyukon chief shrugged, motioned, and Loon-cry was brought forth.

"Do you wish see this man burned, Kutchin woman?" he asked.

"If Loon-cry agree to be your wife, then you let these two

go free?" she pleaded. "No, I not going to be your woman. Instead, you give Danl-ock freedom, Black Claw too. You burn me instead. I will go to the fire."

Red Bear stared at Loon-cry as though seeing her, actually seeing her for the first time.

"You would do such a thing for a *Whiteman*?" he demanded. "You offer to die for worthless Yengee? Crazy woman, no brain in her head. The Yengee thinks he's great wrestler —Koyukons not strong as he is. I don't want this woman no more. I wrestle the Whiteman, break his back, then cut off his head. After that I kill loudmouth Kutchin also."

"Maybe you don't win," Black Claw said, at the same time grinning from ear to ear. He glanced at Dan, and the two men nodded. For at least a fleeting moment, they realized, they'd achieved the upper hand.

Red Bear studied Loon-cry's fierce eyes, then glanced disdainfully back at his two captives.

"I cut Kutchin's tongue out before I kill him. Okay. If Daniel Locke wins, then all three get freedom. If Yengee loses, he gets burned alive, his woman with him. Then I kill the Kutchin. Does this please you, Loon-cry? All three of you get to crawl through Raven Man's tunnel together."

"You just fell into my hands, Red Bear. Big hands, see? Strong hands. You accept defeat better than Blue Weasel did? Or do your warriors jump me then and stick knives into me, even though I am unarmed?"

The powerful Koyukon laughed.

"Would not even be amusing," he declared. "I am much stronger than you. Look at me, Yengee! I eat Russian flesh— I kill you and eat your brains, only you don't got any. Red Bear of the Koyukons don't burn no woman to death, not one as beautiful as Loon-cry. As for Black Claw, he nothing but noise, just like all his people. Think you outsmart me, Dan Locke? Get me angry? You two like Goddamn mosquitoes, that's all. I change my offer now. You take Loon-cry, Yengee Dan, and you go on foot. After one day I follow you. I come alone. If I catch you, then I kill you and Kutchin both. After that Loon-cry be my third wife, no matter what. She do what I want."

Lucky Dan considered goading the Koyukon into going through with the proposed wrestling match and concluded

against it. The chief had spoken—and he'd committed himself to a contest in which the odds were, if anything, on Dan's
side.

A man had to know when it was time to stop raising the
pot. He'd learned that much, at least, from McLafferty the
gambler that time at Fort Union. And now fate was offering
an open corridor to possible freedom, and a man ought to know
better than to tempt fate.

Lucky Dan, Loon-cry, and Black Claw were given their
freedom. The men's knives, but not their pistols and rifles,
were returned to them.

So far, at least, Red Bear seemed intent upon keeping his
word.

The three were escorted slowly away from the assembly
beside the big fire at village center. They were accompanied
by Honker and Raccoon's Mask, the two Koyukon warriors
carrying fusees pointed directly at their backs, and by a young
boy who carried a spruce pitch torch—the latter hardly necessary, since the summer sky had already lightened to a thin
silver-gray. They passed by the landing where twenty or more
canoes were lined up and on down a trail beside Koyukuk
River.

After perhaps a mile, the escorts halted.

"You got what you want, Luckydan," Honker said. "Maybe
you even humiliate Red Bear in front of his people. Now you
find out if you can keep what you got. Red Bear be after you
tomorrow, just like he say. He catch up okay, then you have
to fight. Nobody else around, just you two an' the chief."

Dan nodded, glanced from one Koyukon to the other.

"Friends," he said. "They don't call me Lucky Dan for
nothing. You tell Red Bear to walk slow. That way I won't be
obliged to hurt him."

Raccoon Mask shook his head.

"Good-bye, Luckydan," he said.

With that, the two warriors and the boy with the torch
turned away in the direction of their village.

"Now what we going to do, Danl-ock?" Loon-cry asked.
For a long moment she continued to act like one who dreamed,
but then she threw herself into her husband's arms and began
to sob. Her entire body was trembling.

And Dan realized that he, too, was trembling. The two of them clung to one another for a long moment.

"Let's leave, hokay?" Black Claw said. "Or maybe you think we ought go back there one more time. Just startin' to get comfortable in Goddam village. Maybe want be big friends with Red Bear."

"Matter of fact," Dan said, now holding Loon-cry out at arm's length and assessing the reality of her actually being alive, "here's what I think. We're not heading down the Koyukuk toward Nulato. That's what Red Bear's expecting. This thing has turned into a kind of game for him. Just you, Black Claw. We part company, go in separate directions—that way old skunk-bear can't follow both of us. He'll see the sign, of course, track after me an' Loon-cry. Old Chief, you get the hell on back to Nulato and your new lady, Salmon Berry. If Loon-cry and I don't show up after a decent interval, you drift down to Ikogmut to get Naomi Walks-Between-Worlds. You and Salmon Berry and Snow Flower raise her as though she were your own daughter, just the way we agreed before. You make a hell of a grandfather. Don't rightly know if I could have whipped the Koyukon or not, but I've got a hunch I might be able to outrun him—at least if I can out-think him, use the old brain a bit. He's a cagy son of a bitch, but maybe. . . . Loon-cry and me, we're heading for Unalakleet and on to St. Mike. And Gawddamn it, Black Claw, don't double back on me this time. Our little girl needs parents, no matter what else happens. One way or another, she deserves the chance to walk between those two worlds, just like her name says."

Black Claw studied Dan's face and then turned to Loon-cry, gave her a big hug.

"You alive, all right, little Loon girl," he grinned. "No Goddam ghost, hokay. Honest God human flesh. You take care of dumbass White devil. After all this, don' want nothin' else bad to happen."

Then he shook Dan's hand, nodded in apparent high spirits, turned precipitantly away as though fearing Dan might change his mind, and began to jog easily down the Koyukuk River trail, at length vanishing from sight among the trees.

"Your slave, Loon-girl, is an extremely complex son of a bitch. At least, I think he is. Let's get moving, Lady Lazarus."

"You forget my name, Danl-ock? Think I'm dead, an'
sleeping with other women?"

Locke turned back to her.

In the forest all about them, owls began to call. Their cries
filled the thin silver of half-light.

13

Running from Red Bear

The Arctic sun was an angry yellow hole at sky's center,
and Locke, sweating profusely, could only estimate the temperature at ninety or more—the engulfing, muggy heat of Far
North summer.

Nonetheless, Dan and Loon-cry kept up a tireless pace,
taking full advantage of twenty-two hours of daylight and stopping to rest only as necessity demanded. They followed upstream along a tributary river that flowed northeastward toward
its confluence with the Koyukuk. The trail was one commonly
used by the Koyukons when either whim or the necessities of
trade required them to venture across to Unalakleet or to Redoubt St. Michael further south.

*One day's head start—that's what he said. And of course
I believe the lying swamphawg. Koyukon chief speak with straight
tongue, but maybe words come out crooked as hell anyway.
It's two hundred miles to Unalakleet, more or less, and once
Loon and I reach the pass below Debauch Mountain, then it's
relatively familiar country to me—in any case, I'll know where
I'm going from there. Between here and the mountain, however, that's a different matter. The son of a bitch Red Bear's
on our trail already, I can feel it in my bones—but at least
Charlie-the-Claw should be in the clear. Gawddamn it, a footrace or a wit race, then. Don't know about the first—he probably knows every inch of this terrain. But just possibly, with*

a bit of Missouri common sense, we can win the second. Turn north, cross over the hills to Kateel River. . . . Ambush him if necessary, jump down out of a tree onto his back, tear off one of his arms and beat him to death with it.

"You want to go wrong direction, Danl-ock? We never get to the ocean that way—Koyukons tell me. . . ."

Dan nodded, winked.

"But maybe we can fox him, Loon-love. Better that Red Bear's ahead of us than behind us. Track the bad bear, don't let him track you: advice an old mountaineer gave me a few years ago—after he got his ear bitten off by a griz."

"Not better just go the opposite way? Then we don't have to worry about Red Bear at all. We goin' to sleep pretty soon, ain't we? Don' think I can keep going. . . ."

"Can you hold up a few more hours? Red Bear didn't wait—I can feel it. Told us a full day to give us a false sense of security. I can feel the bastard out there behind us, and not very far, either."

Loon-cry nodded, and without further talk the man and woman turned away from the Koyukon trail, wading against the current of a fast-flowing lateral stream that flowed down from rolling tundra highlands to the north. The water was cold, numbing their feet and legs, and progress was extremely slow.

Dan knew that even the purpose of this tactic was highly questionable. While Red Bear might well simply pass by in his haste to overtake them, assuming his quarry had continued along the main way, once he'd concluded otherwise and doubled back to check carefully for sign, he'd no doubt realize what was afoot.

A mile or so upstream, Lucky Dan and Loon-cry left the water and moved ahead at a fast walk. When a bare, rocky slope presented itself, they angled upward toward the ridge-crest.

It was twenty miles, as Dan calculated matters, over to the Kateel, a stream he could only hope ran more or less parallel to the Koyukon Trail.

Halfway across the range of hills, exhaustion and hunger overtook them, and Dan realized further progress was impossible until they'd managed to find something to eat and had been able to sleep for a few hours at least.

A small stream meandered through some broad meadows, and in its waters Loon-cry discovered several small chub hanging nearly motionless in the churning current. Locke lay down at the stream's edge and reached slowly, slowly into the water, placing a hand beneath one of the fish. In imitation of a bear, he attempted to slap one of the chub out of the shallow current, but without luck. All the fish darted away upstream—uncertain what kind of creature was after them, but certain something was.

"Man'd think you sons-of-bitches don't want to get eaten," he muttered. "Too damn dumb to recognize your proper destiny."

Dan continued his efforts with increasing frustration until at last, his leathers soaked and the fish scattered and laughing at him from hiding spots among rocks and weeds, he lay back on the bank cursing his own clumsiness.

Loon-cry sat several yards away beside a clump of willow brush, working intently at some object in her hands.

"Looks like fin-people ain't on the menu today, Loon-gal. You Injuns are supposed to have all kinds of tricks—you've told me that yourself, many times. So. You know about some roots or berries or grubs or somethin' you can dig up? I'm ready for grass stew or damned near anything else."

"You mean you don' scare those fish to death yet, Danlock? Whiteman always do thing the hard way. Injuns sneaky, okay. Here."

She held up what appeared to be a large, loosely woven basket of willow shoots anchored to a hoop of the same material. Dan stared for a moment before it dawned on him what Loon-cry had manufactured.

"Fish net?" he said. "Oh, hell, that ain't going to work. . . ."

But with the aid of the crude interweaving of twigs, and with Dan slogging up the stream to where Loon-cry waited with her willow mesh, they managed to scoop out a dozen chub, half of which they devoured raw, not wanting to risk even a small fire until after the time of gray twilight set in—no sense, after all, in advertising their whereabouts.

"Will Red Bear come alone?" Loon-cry asked.

"No doubt you know the gentleman better than I do, Loon-cry. But my guess is he'll stick to that part of his word, at least. Hell, he knows the lay of the land, and we don't. And he'll have a fusee or my Colt Walker at the very least, while all I've got is my knife. Truth to tell, I hope the thick-necked bastard brings my Hawken along. This coon wants his damned guns returned. Feel naked as a camp-robber jay without 'em. Right now I'm half of a mind to double back and track him. . . ."

"Why you say that? Shoot us from way off."

"Get right down to it, the only damned chance we've really got is for me to mug that bastard and take whatever firearm he comes equipped with. Got to think out a plan, though. The problem with survival in this country is that a man has to keep thinking all the time."

Dan wiped at his mouth, took Loon-cry in his arms, and kissed her.

"By Gawd, it's good to have ye back from the dead, little one. You've got no idea just how absolute miserable I've been—like a little kid lost out in the woods, only there wasn't any way of finding my way home because there wasn't any home left. Just me and Naomi Walks-Between-Worlds and that worthless old bastard, Black Claw. I saw you down, bleeding, not moving. . . . Then meeting up with Red Bear's men over to St. Mike and then racing back to the Koyukon village for no more reason than the words of some drunks and my own desire for it to be true and a Gawddamned prayer that they were telling this child the truth. It's all like a dream, and probably I'll wake up directly and find out I'm alone again."

Suddenly Locke felt like a child once more, a child on the verge of tears.

"No dream," Loon-cry replied softly. "I know you find out somehow, return for me. I tried to run away once, soon as I strong enough to do it. Red Bear come after me, make me go back to his village. Or maybe he kill us both. Then what happen to our little one? She's safe? With Snow Flower and Rooshian medicine man? You give him money to take care of her? Ain't right, how all this happen. Goddam Raven Man. . . ."

"Yep, if Red Bear catches up to us, could be it's all over," Dan said. "Maybe not, though. He can't be any tougher than your basic grizzly. Considering what I stand to lose, I'd say Red Bear's got his hands full. A knife's a hell of a lot better than no weapon at all. There's a chance, there's a chance. Only a coward or a damned fool gives up before he's whipped. That's what my daddy told me, an' I've lived by it ever since. This

game ain't over yet, no sir. But we've got to keep our wits
about us—best if we could ambush the son of a bitch. Yep,
I'm sorely tempted to leave you here and backtrack—lie in
wait for Uncle Red Bear. The element of surprise—that evens
the odds a bit at times. I thought my luck had run out, but
maybe I just didn't have enough faith in the medicine. . . ."

"He wants me to see him kill you, just you an' him fight.
You wrestle Blue Weasel an' win. Red Bear, he talks about
that—like he don' believe it really happened. He want to
wrestle with you, Danl-ock, only he don' want whole village
watching. That's why he let us go, with him hunting us."

"Guess that's it, all right."

"He's strong."

"Yep. I could see that, no question. I play by Texas rules,
though, when the stakes are high enough."

"Tex-as rules?"

"Another way of sayin' *no rules at all.*"

"Didn't know about rules. What are they, Danl-ock?"

"Beats the hell out of me," he grinned. "Let's talk about
something else."

"What?" she asked.

"Lying down—together. Might be our last chance this
side of the ghostly river."

"Make . . . love?"

"Unless you're not interested."

"Interested," she said, pressing her mouth against his,
"but this ain't very good place. Mosquitoes startin' to get thick."

"Ain't those young eagles? Anyhow, I thought the varmints only bothered Whitemen." He laughed.

"These the size of woodpeckers, anyhow," she replied,
fanning the whining insects away from her face.

The sun's red smear slowly dropped behind long ridges
to the northwest, and the day's heat dissipated rapidly. For a
time a burning crescent slid along the horizon, turning long,
thin bands of mottled clouds to blazing crimson so that the
mountains themselves seemed afire, at length disappearing,
and grayness flooded over high tundra splatched with ragged
spruce groves.

Lucky Dan and Loon-cry, half leaning on one another,
worked their way up through low growth of heather to the foot

of some free-standing boulders, and here they rested for a time before building a small fire. They roasted their remaining fish, ate, and afterward fell into one another's arms—hungry now for yet a different sort of nourishment, the result of a long, hopeless interval of denial enforced by black despair.

"This time I bite little salmon's head off," Loon-cry murmured, unlacing his leathers as she did so. "Crazy fish. All hard. Stands up on its tail I guess. Only got one eye, though. . . ."

"A damned big fish, I'll have you know. Biggest anywhere along the Lot of Water. But if you bite me, by Gawd, I swear I'll tongue your honey-pot until she's having twelve kinds of fit, and after that I'll hump you like any bull moose with his cow."

"Big talk, very small salmon. Good one though. I like it. You fall asleep when Loon-cry's finished. Always big talk, Danlock. Be quiet now . . . if you can. . . . Don' want no roaring an' snorting like bull moose when he's crazy."

Lucky Dan groaned as she took him into her mouth, and he reached forward to place his hands to either side of her head.

A sensation of trickling fire began to mix with the ache that tormented him.

It was something he never in the world supposed he'd ever experience again—something he knew he'd never wish to do with any other woman. It was crazy, crazy, but it was sacred, too. It was . . . Loon-cry, and all the confused madness that he could only feel when he was around her, a madness he'd supposed he'd lost forever.

By what miracle had she managed to come back from Raven Man's tunnel?

At length they slept—tangled in one another's arms and perhaps even sharing one another's dreams. Utter exhaustion flooded over them, and time itself seemed to cease.

When they awoke to brilliant sunlight, they perceived that perhaps a thousand black-headed geese were swarming over the broad meadows down below where they lay, their arms still about one another.

But the interlude was over, and within a short while they were again trudging forward, their energies renewed by sleep but their limbs only grudgingly obeying the combined will power that drove them—that and perhaps a phantom of hope that they might yet be able to share their lives, to raise their child, to grow old in one another's company. . . .

They reached Kateel River and moved on upstream—not quite so hurriedly now, but keeping to a steady, distance-devouring pace. Late in the oppressive heat of afternoon Dan clubbed a fat, scuttling porcupine to death, carefully gutting and skinning the creature. Loon-cry dug some camas roots, and when twilight descended once again and they felt it safe to build a small fire, they were able to enjoy a full meal.

The river continued to pour down from the southwest, and Locke was now virtually certain its course was almost precisely parallel to the stream along which the Koyukon Trail ran.

He attempted to imagine himself in Red Bear's place—would he have crossed over to the Kateel or simply have continued on toward Unalakleet? At some point beyond Debauch Mountain, without question, Locke and Loon-cry would be obliged to drop back onto the Koyukon Trail—or else to cut directly westward in hope of finding the village of Skaktoolik, close by Cape Denbigh—if, indeed, he'd sufficiently memorized the details of that Russian map he'd seen in Pieter Dobshansky's office at Redoubt St. Michael.

On the fourth day since their departure from the Koyukon village, Lucky Dan and Loon-cry reached the Kateel's headwaters and then emerged onto a broad, rolling, barren plateau from which rose a mountain Dan presumed had to be Debauch. From this point they moved off southward through long stretches of uneven ground spattered with heather, fireweed, glacier lilies, and Arctic poppies.

Within about three hours they reached the trail Dan had taken on his forced march from Unalakleet across to Nulato.

More or less certain of his precise location for the first time in several days, Dan chose to move a mile or so back away from the overland route, and the two spent a chilly night without benefit of fire—in all probability a needless precaution under the circumstances. But with potential refuge in an Eskimo village perhaps no more than a day and a half's journey ahead, the two agreed, it was better to take no unnecessary risks.

"You stay here in the morning, Loon-love, and I'll do a little scouting along the trail—see if I can determine whether the big bear's been along this way as yet. Maybe we've actually lost him—maybe not. Hell, it could be that he never really intended to follow us at all. Just his way of encouraging us to get the hell out of his territory—an' don't look back. He's a complicated son of a bitch. Could have put this child under any one of three times—starting with me doubling back to bury my friend Hans when I talked Murray into letting me take a fur brigade downriver into Koyukon lands. Get right down to it, why the hell hasn't he killed me? It ain't like we're old friends, after all, or long-lost relatives, or anything like that. So maybe you and I have been running ourselves crazy for no reason at all. . . ."

Loon-cry shook her head.

"He's out there somewhere, Danl-ock. I can feel his presence. Red Bear closer now than before. I don' know. Better we stay together. What if he's right behind? You leave, then he comes in. . . . You come back, I can't warn you."

"A distinct possibility. If he's close, like you say, I wish he'd show himself. With all this running an' constant looking over our shoulders, the truth is I'm starting to get a bit riled. Time to have it out, one way or t'other. Give me half a chance, and I'll plant the square-faced son of a bitch, I swear it."

It was midmorning when Lucky Dan and Loon-cry awoke. Virtually certain he detected a faint odor of woodsmoke, Locke walked quickly to the summit of a dolmen and scanned the visible area—but could see nothing. He returned to Loon-cry, gave her assurance that he'd been mistaken. He took a few mouthfuls of their remaining porcupine flesh, embraced Loon-cry, and strode off toward the low point in the ridge where the Koyukon Trail passed over the mountains.

Within two hours he was back.

"Nary so much as a sign of 'im. I think we've been running from a phantom. Looks like the way's clear to Unalakleet. Let's move out while the moving's good. It's two days journey to Redoubt St. Michael, and I've got letters of credit there. We'll take passage on a Russian-American supply frigate bound for the Kuikpak delta and points south, hitch a ride with a bidarra upriver, and get Naomi at Ikogmut. . . ."

Loon-cry threw herself into her husband's arms.

"Then what we do, Danl-ock? Find Black Claw an' Salmon Berry, then go back up river to Fort Youcan—or maybe go where you tell me—place where big river don' freeze?"

"Whatever my lady says. I love this crazy land, sixty below and all, but the place went empty when I thought you were dead, Loon. Now that you're back from . . . well, I guess things are beginning to shine again. But there are other mountains, other rivers. Hell, I'm up for a change, whatever you want. We can start over—maybe even do some prospecting for gold in California. Places down there where it don't even snow, just like I told you, and she's by-Gawd a genuine state of the union now. Maybe we could homestead some land even—and raise cows."

"I go where you go, Danl-ock," Loon-cry replied. "What are these things, *cows?*"

Dan chuckled.

"Like tame caribou—well, sort of like that. Lots of things you don't know about, Loon-gal. But you're willing to go anywhere I want? For a fact now? Well, in that case, let's hotfoot it for Unalakleet. . . ."

"How far?"

Lucky Dan laughed, squinted off at the horizon.

"Forty miles—not an inch farther. Lass, you've got my word on it."

"Two days of walking."

"Nothing to 'er. Hell, I'm just starting to get fond of this shank's mare business."

"Say what makes sense. I don' understand. . . ."

"Keep an eye out for friendly porcupines and circling vultures, Lu-lu-loon. We're going to need a few quick meals along the way. Truth is, I've gotten fond of eating, too."

A day and a half later they crested a mountain above Unalakleet and from there were able to look down on the broad gray waters of Norton Sound—now perhaps no more than ten miles distant.

The two embraced, and Lucky Dan let out a whoop.

"We've made it, by Gawd. Ye up for a little downhill jaunt?"

Loon-cry smiled, her deep brown eyes glinting sunlight.

Hand in hand and all but skipping like children, the two hurried downslope toward the little river that would, within a few more miles, merge its current into heaving salt water

"What take you so long?"

The words hung in the air for a long moment, and Locke immediately stepped in front of Loon-cry and drew his knife.

It was Red Bear, chief of the Koyukons, and he was holding a pistol—Locke's Colt Walker.

Lucky Dan stared at his antagonist, still only half believing. Then he nodded.

"It's time to wrestle," he said, his voice soft and sounding, it seemed to Loon-cry, actually somewhat relieved—perhaps even eager for this delayed conflict to begin.

Dan stripped off his leather jacket and shirt, all but ignoring Red Bear, and proceeded to hand both his garments and his knife to Loon-cry. He turned then, approached the Koyukon chief.

"Not wish to use the knife?" Red Bear asked, grinning. "Just your strength against mine, then. Is that what you wish, Yengee Boston?"

"Wouldn't have it any other way, you no-neck, fat-bellied bastard."

Red Bear burst out laughing.

"You have long neck," he replied. "I break it—after that cut your head off and stick it on pole. Ravens pick out your eyes."

The powerful Indian stripped to the waist, placed his clothing across a windfall larch and hung his sheath knife and the pistol from a broken-off limb.

Then the two men, without further words, began to circle one another.

Their initial embraces proved inconclusive, however, as neither man was able to manipulate the other to any particular advantage. Nonetheless, Dan was easily able to determine that the Koyukon chief was indeed a formidable opponent —strong like the bear for which he was named, fierce, a pure warrior, one who loved combat and lived in constant anticipation of it. If Dan had previously entertained any skeptical doubt as to the validity of his opponent's reputation, the doubt vanished.

Red Bear, eyes wide and teeth bared, stalked forward.

"*Texas rules*, chief," Dan said, spitting out the words.

With that, and setting his weight carefully, he drove his fist flush into the Koyukon's face and sent the astonished Red Bear to the ground, where he remained for a moment on hands and knees, stunned by the surprise blow and shaking his head.

Dan leaped forward, delivering a hard kick to the side of the Indian's head and flipping him over onto his back. In an instant he was astride the man, one knee across his opponent's throat.

"I've won!" Lucky Dan bellowed. "Red Bear, you worthless son of a bitch, are you man enough to keep your word?"

The Koyukon's bruised face was now a mask of rage. Suddenly he twisted about, hurling Dan forward and onto his side. In that instant Red Bear was on his feet and lurching toward the windfall larch from which his knife and cap-and-ball pistol were hanging.

The weapons, however, were no longer there.

Dan set himself, turned his gaze toward where Loon-cry was standing, her hands on her hips.

If she ain't got the damned knife and pistol, then where in blazes . . . ?

Black Claw stepped out from behind a screen of willow brush, Dan's Hawken rifle and Colt Walker pistol in one hand, the extra knife safely tucked under his belt, and a Hudson's Bay fusee held in the other, its gray-blue muzzle pointed directly at Red Bear.

"Whitemen and Koyukons both very stupid, just like I always think," the old scar-faced warrior laughed. "Forget all about me. I act like camp-robber jay—find Koyukon's stuff, take it. Probably don't know how to shoot Luckydan's rifle anyway. Hokay, Loon-cry? Maybe debt all paid off after this, eh? Now I kill Red Bear, go back, be chief of his village. Kill Luckydan too, though, avenge dead son even if he ain't no good, marry Loon-cry myself. Then I have three wives, even if I only got one good eye. Hell, maybe marry Snow Flower too. That make four wives. Old guys like me, we the best husbands anyhow."

"Where in hell'd you come from, you miserable thief?" Dan demanded.

"Easy. Wait for Red Bear to take trail across hills, then

follow. Come to place where you an' Loon-cry wade up little creek. After that I follow you two—just keep back, out of sight. Keep watchin', all time watchin'. Pretty smart, hokay?"

At that moment Red Bear, screaming incoherently, lunged toward Black Claw, the Koyukon no doubt fully expecting to be shot to death but willing to risk it in the hope of taking the Kutchin when he least expected it.

Black Claw waited for the last possible instant and pivoted on one heel, then turned about as Red Bear flopped heavily to the ground, knocking the wind out of himself. Then, still fighting for his breath, he rose slowly to one knee, his eyes blazing the defiance of fierce pride. "Goddam ugly Kutchin," Red Bear said. "Figured you run like hell to Nulato."

Black Claw shrugged.

"No fun that way," he said. "You got problem breathin'?"

Loon-cry stepped forward, studied Black Claw's expression, and then turned toward Red Bear, who was now back on his feet and clearly ready to continue the conflict at the first opportune moment.

"Red Bear," Loon-cry said, "you made the medicine woman save my life once. Now I will spare yours by ordering Black Claw not to kill you. Return to your people and tell them whatever you wish."

"I still gotta do what you say?" Black Claw grinned.

"Yes. You must always do what I tell you."

"Let's finish this damned wrestling match," Lucky Dan suggested. "Hell, Red Bear, you're not tough at all. One of these days one of your own young bucks is going to take you on and tie you in knots. You're not much more than a lot of noise."

The American was poised, obviously ready and willing to continue.

Red Bear studied Locke and his two confederates for a moment, began to laugh, shrugged, and gave the North Country hand-sign indicating submission to a superior enemy.

"Got old an' weak all of a sudden," the Koyukon said. "You kill me now or give me back my clothing and weapons. I return to my village. You win, Yengee Boston. Brave an' stupid ain't same thing. Remember I tell you this. . . ."

Epilogue

Up from Apoon Mouth

A bidarra laden with needed supplies had come upriver, the ungainly sealhide canoe launched from the trawler *Stahri Omahrahv* offshore of Kuikpak Delta under the command of a Boston, his crew consisting of half a dozen Creoles—a commission, as it were, granted by Pieter Dobshansky himself, the Russian-American Company chief agent. The craft proceeded into the river's Apoon Channel and so continued inland through tundra barrens to the mission post of Ikogmut.

The Yankee in question was none other than Lucky Dan Locke, acting supply officer for Russian operations along the Kuikpak.

Using numerous repetitions of the phrases *"Ehtah krahrahsho,* it is beautiful," and "Lord be with you, my son," Father Georgi listened in undisguised amazement to Dan Locke's tale of Loon-cry's apparent return from death and Locke's subsequent conflict with the dreaded Koyukons and overland flight and final confrontation.

Nonetheless the priest experienced hesitancy, genuine hesitancy, about returning the infant Naomi to her father and the woman Dan claimed to be the child's mother—indeed, he almost felt he was betraying the little girl, allowing her to be taken back into the unrelieved darkness of native animistic superstition and hence, no doubt, to be deprived of the light of true salvation.

Furthermore, the priest reflected, he was going to miss the occasional company of Snow Flower, a young woman of whom he'd grown genuinely fond and to whom he'd been attempting to render the mysteries of Christian salvation.

160

On the other hand, Loon-cry's self-evident love for the child she thought she had lost gave him the feeling that all would be well—as well as it ever could be for a human creature. He placed two sets of rosary beads into the mother's hand, touched momentarily at the small crucifix said to have been given her by the unfortunate Vasily Deriabin, nodded.

So miraculous a return to life! That portion of Locke's account was nearly beyond the holy man's comprehension. A Koyukon medicine woman, so the story went, had entered into a trance state and had sought out Loon-cry's wandering soul and had supposedly brought it back? Surely, then, the attractive young woman had not been dead at all—it was merely that this American, Lucky Dan Locke, had been fooled and then spirited out of the Koyukon village. Possibly the shaman had even administered some sort of native opiate to Loon-cry who had then fallen into a coma that mimicked death itself.

When one was dead, after all, one was dead. . . .

Stories of this sort, forever arising in one village or another and flying on the wings of rumor up and down the length of the muddy Kuikpak, ate at the very roots of the Faith that such men as he and Netzvetov sought to instill within the unruly minds of these, their savage flock.

No, it was not even that the husband believed in the miraculous—for his was an innocent and non-mystical nature. If anything, Locke explained the whole thing simply in terms of *luck*. It was Georgi himself who responded to the tale as though he were hearing of Lazarus being healed by an unknown Physician.

Now, however, Snow Flower and the American and his friends were gone, back onto the big river and bound for the abandoned Russian trading post at the village of Núlato, more than three hundred miles upstream—Daniel Locke and his Kutchin wife and their little daughter and their astonishingly ugly companion, one-eyed Black Claw, who professed loyalty to Loon-cry as though she were the Holy Madonna and the next moment insisted that every *White Devil* along the entire length of the Lot of Water should be beheaded, the *God men* most of all.

Such individuals, Father Georgi concluded, should never be trusted. What sort of impious barbarian, after all, would refer to the respected Aleut-Russian Father Netzvetov, one who had devoted his existence to the improvement of his people, as "Goddam Gossack Devil"?

But now they were out on the glittering, sunlit water, moving off toward Nulato.

The priest raised his arm, waved.

"*Dah sveedahneeyah!*" he called out, "Good-bye! Go with God!"

Father Georgi turned away from the river and walked slowly toward the little onion dome-topped Christian church perched there in the midst of savagery. It was, he concluded, doubtless the finest assignment a priest might have.

Back in the tundra barrens to the south of the Kuikpak, the wolves were calling—calling to one another, singing, singing in the full light of midday.

Yes, Father Georgi reflected, he would definitely miss Snow Flower. Perhaps, at some future time, he would himself find reason to venture up to Nulato.

Naomi Walks-Between-World's eyes were rich brown, just like her mother's—and the child, somewhat past her first birthday, was beautifully formed. Loon-cry held her, perhaps, far more than necessary, speaking to her in Kutchin dialect, a language the child could hardly have understood.

Dan and Black Claw sat in the prow, and while the old warrior rattled on to the Creole oarsmen about one thing or another, Dan stared at his wife and child—and at Snow Flower, the latter breast-feeding her own little one. He breathed deeply and grinned in spite of himself.

Loon-cry was telling Naomi a tale about how Beaver-Man and Wolverine-Man were thirsty in the long-ago time, and Beaver-Man created the Lot of Water so that they might have something to drink.

Thoughts of California gold or of farmland near the growing city close by where the Missouri and Mississippi Rivers converged—such contemplations were far from his mind. *Come wind, come snow, come sixty below temperatures—what the hell?* He and Loon-cry and Naomi and Black Claw and the old reprobate's new lady friend (presuming Salmon Berry and her daughter-in-law could be convinced to migrate upriver), they were all by-Gawd heading back to the far interior. They were bound for Fort Youcan.

"Not a bad place, when a man gets right down to 'er," Lucky Dan mused.

Sunlight on the river ahead of them refracted into a million tiny cups of golden fire, while ducks and loons were skimming low to the water. Ravens drifted overhead, herons and cranes were pumping through the air, and far, far up above the rolling spruce and larch forests of the taiga, eagles described long arcs against endless blue.

Unseen, gliding upstream against the Lot of Water's relentless gray-green current, salmon were already making their way inevitably back to the redds where they had hatched and found life.

Things were, Lucky Dan reflected, exactly as they should be—even though that *should be* often didn't correspond to the urgings of human desire.

Esnaih. Always got to keep moving. Gawddamn big land. Ours. . . .

A Proud People In a Harsh Land

THE SPANISH BIT SAGA

Set on the Great Plains of America in the early 16th century, Don Coldsmith's acclaimed series recreates a time, a place and a people that have been nearly lost to history. With the advent of the Spaniards, the horse culture came to the people of the Plains. In THE SPANISH BIT SAGA we see history in the making through the eyes of the proud Native Americans who lived it.

THE SPANISH BIT SAGA
Don Coldsmith

☐ BOOK 1: TRAIL OF THE SPANISH
  BIT   26397 $2.95
☐ BOOK 2: THE ELK-DOG
  HERITAGE   26412 $2.95
☐ BOOK 3: FOLLOW THE WIND   26806 $2.95
☐ BOOK 4: BUFFALO MEDICINE   26938 $2.95
☐ BOOK 5: MAN OF THE SHADOWS 27067 $2.95

"An American original."
—*The New York Times Book Review*
"Leonard writes tough."—*The Chicago Sun-Times*
"The finest thriller writer alive."—*The Village Voice*

ELMORE LEONARD

Whether writing about life in the fast lane or on the rugged American frontier, there is no writer quite like Elmore Leonard. Pick up all these thrilling adventures at your local bookstore—or use the handy coupon below for ordering.

Special Offer
Buy a Bantam Book
for only 50¢.

Now you can have Bantam's catalog filled with hundreds of titles plus take advantage of our unique and exciting bonus book offer. A special offer which gives you the opportunity to purchase a Bantam book for only 50¢. Here's how!

By ordering any five books at the regular price per order, you can also choose any other single book listed (up to a $5.95 value) for just 50¢. Some restrictions do apply, but for further details why not send for Bantam's catalog of titles today!

Just send us your name and address and we will send you a catalog!